D1052966

THE SECRET BEAU

Other books by Annette Mahon:

Above the Rainbow
Chase Your Dream
Just Friends
Lei of Love
Maui Rose
A Phantom Death
The Secret Admirer
The Secret Wedding
The Secret Santa

THE SECRET BEAU

•

Annette Mahon

AVALON BOOKS
NEW YORK

Library of Congress Catalog Card Number: 2004090291
ISBN 0-8034-9663-X

Published by Thomas Bouregy & Co., Inc.
160 Madison Avenue, New York, NY 10016

PRINTED IN THE UNITED STATES OF AMERICA
ON ACID-FREE PAPER
BY HADDON CRAFTSMEN, BLOOMSBURG, PENNSYLVANIA

For Deni, Garda, Harriet, Lillian, Mary Jo, Pam, Sherry-Anne, and Terey—my fellow muses. For all your support and encouragement; for listening to the agonies as well as the bliss of creation . . . mahalo.

Chapter One

"Man, it takes a load of courage to do that."

Blinking tear-filled eyes at the touching scene that had just played out before her, Kim Ascension wondered which of the men around her made the comment she'd just overheard. Whoever it was, he had not denigrated the beautiful way that Ben Mendoza had proposed to Mele Pitman in front of the whole town of Malino. No, she was sure she heard admiration in that voice—admiration for a man who was brave enough to be so romantic. Perhaps from one who was not so brave.

Despite her tears, Kim was still smiling at the beautiful couple. Ben had gotten down on one knee to propose—right there in front of everyone at the town Christmas party. It was always the event of the year in Malino, but this year's party would be talked about for the next fifty years. Maybe more.

Ben was so romantic, Kim could hardly believe he was for real. But there he was, kissing his new fiancée. She could see some of the younger boys making faces and gagging motions about the whole scene. They were much too cool for this stuff, though they knew how to cheer on the kissing part. If Ben wasn't such a handsome, macho *paniolo*, she was sure the older guys would be making derogatory noises too.

But no one dared impugn the masculinity of the hard-working cowboy. He might be new to their town, but he'd managed to fit in quickly with his serious work ethic and his sincere love for their own Mele. The only grumbling Kim heard came from those who were afraid he was setting a new, and higher, standard that would be difficult for the rest of them to meet. Kim had to smile as she watched a few of the younger men shifting uncomfortably from foot to foot as they eyed their girlfriends in troubled silence.

Kim heard the voice again and looked around. She really wanted to know who that was. Probably one of the married men, who had proposed in a traditional, private manner.

Moving toward the voice, she listened carefully. Finally, she was able to pinpoint the speaker. Blinking rapidly to clear the last of her sentimental tears, Kim checked him out. There was something familiar about him, she thought.

Kim continued to look, unaware that she might be staring. The man was young, probably only a little older than she. And he was tall, definitely over six feet and maybe as much as six foot two. His frame was lean and athletic—the kind of guy who'd played basketball in high school or had run track. His thick wavy hair was a brown so dark it was almost black, and worn too long for a military or professional man. His eyes were almond-shaped and almost as dark as his hair. Kind of a young Keanu Reeves with a taller, leaner body, she thought.

But his face was *so* familiar . . .

He reminded her of someone, someone she went to high school with. It took Kim a moment to remember. *Greg*

Yamamoto. At least, his face reminded her of Greg Yamamoto.

Greg had definitely not been the athletic type, though, at least not in high school. He was a very nice guy, several years ahead of her in school and desperate to be a veterinarian. He loved all the sciences and was great at math, too. But he'd had problems with his English papers.

The memories brought a smile to Kim's lips. She still remembered the thrill she'd felt when her teacher asked her if she would be willing to tutor someone in English. A senior boy! As a freshman, it was something that had both excited and scared her, especially when she heard Greg was the one the teacher wanted her to help. They lived fairly close and she'd known exactly who he was. He wasn't so tall then, or so buff. He was lean and rangy, the kind of guy who looked like he'd suddenly gotten his height and wasn't quite sure how to handle it. And he'd been a classic science nerd, spending a lot of time in the library working on the school computers.

Kim took another look. It *was* Greg Yamamoto, she was sure of it. Come to think of it, she'd heard that he was back in town. She didn't know how she'd managed to miss seeing him; maybe he did his banking online.

Someone had started the room singing "Hawaii Aloha" to end the evening, and everyone had taken hold of a neighbor's hand. Kim regretted that she wasn't close enough to be holding Greg's, but she was still able to see him from her position in the giant circle. *And did he ever look terrific*.

How had the skinny, nerdy teenager she remembered become such a hunk? He could have traded in his glasses for contacts, of course, but he must have grown a few more inches and gotten serious about working out.

Whatever he'd done, Greg looked great—with a capital G.

Once the song was finished, and people began to gather up their things, Kim inched her way over to the man who had caught her attention.

"Greg? Is that you?"

The tall young man turned. He smiled.

Wow. Kim's breath swooshed out in a quiet rush. Had she thought he looked good when she'd first spotted him? The smile turned his face from good-looking to dazzlingly attractive. Aunty Liliuokalani, rushing by on urgent business, couldn't resist a glance at him and an approving smile for Kim.

"Kim Ascension." Greg gathered her into a hug, kissing her swiftly on the cheek. "Aloha. What are you doing these days?"

Kim managed a shrug, trying for nonchalant, with effort. His friendly hug had produced a riot of sensations, most of them exciting and all of them surprising.

What was she doing these days? When not having strange reactions to old high school friends?

Not much, she wanted to say. But that wouldn't be right. She was still working at the bank, just as she'd done for the six years since her high school graduation. She had a college degree in business, with a major in finance, but she was still a teller at Statewide Bank in tiny Malino. Still lived with her mother in the house she grew up in. She'd heard that Greg had graduated from the University of Hawaii at Manoa and was now a veterinarian. Word was that he'd wanted to stay in Honolulu and work in a practice that was limited to small pets. There were rumors of a girlfriend too, a city girl. But then his mother became ill, and he moved back to Malino and joined the practice of their only other vet, an occasion that everyone called a great blessing. The local vet, Lawrence DeMello, was near retirement age, but had been reluctant to close the animal clinic he'd started years before. Not many young men wanted to work in a small practice in a small town. They had to doctor the ranch and farm animals too, not just the town's cats and dogs.

Kim managed to summon a smile. It wasn't too difficult, not with that fine-looking smile still aimed at her. Her arms and cheek still tingled from his friendly greeting.

"You mean you don't know?" She laughed. It was the blessing and the curse of living in a small town—everyone knew everything about everybody. "I'm head teller over at Statewide."

She knew how to put a positive spin on her job, even if she often felt frustrated by it.

"Yeah, I guess I knew you were over at the bank," he admitted. "But, head teller . . . good for you."

There was a short pause, and Kim noticed his eyes cloud over, perhaps with pain.

"So you stayed in town. I'm just now beginning to appreciate what we have here." His hand gestured toward the room at large.

Most of Malino's past and present lingered in the high school gym. The town Christmas party was over, but people were reluctant to leave. It was the most anticipated event in Malino all year, easily beating out the Fourth of July rodeo and even the King Kamehameha Day Parade and picnic. Everyone attended the Malino Christmas party; even people who had moved away returned with their spouses, children, and grandchildren. It was the event of the year, and this year it had been better than ever.

Every attendee would remember this year's party for years to come. Ben Mendoza, who had inherited his great-uncle's ranch, had used the children's gift-giving time to announce to the world that he wanted to marry the town's favorite waitress, Mele Pitman. Despite the cynical comments she'd heard from some of the men, Kim knew that, like herself, all the women found the whole thing terribly exciting and incredibly romantic.

"It's been something, hasn't it?" she said to fill the silence.

Greg nodded, though Kim could see he was uncomfortable talking about romance. Typical guy, she thought. They never wanted to get near anything emotional or sentimental.

"All I can say is, that Ben is one brave guy."

Kim frowned. "Brave? Because he wants to marry Mele?" Leave it to a guy to think it took bravery to pop the question.

Greg shook his head. "Brave because he proposed in front of the whole town."

Greg glanced around the gym before turning his gaze back toward Kim. Many families with young children had left, but there were still a lot of people there, especially surrounding Mele and Ben.

"I think it was very romantic." Kim sighed.

"Romantic," Greg muttered. "Bah, humbug."

Kim thought he meant his words to escape unheard, but she'd heard him all right. Another Scrooge in the romance department. How had Mele captured the interest of such a romantic guy? All the men Kim knew seemed to feel the way Greg did.

Still, he was so good-looking, he'd probably be a success with the local women even if he did lack romantic feelings. And, while they hadn't really socialized in high school outside of tutoring, she recalled that he'd been a pretty nice guy. He couldn't have undergone a complete personality change, could he?

Kim caught herself before her active imagination jumped forward, putting the two of them together. She didn't even know if he had a girlfriend or was married, though surely she would have heard if he was.

She turned frantic eyes toward his left hand, feeling the constriction in her chest ease when she saw no ring there. Why was she getting these odd feelings about someone she barely knew? Wasn't it bad enough that her skin had tingled when he'd greeted her with a hug?

With effort, Kim turned her eyes back to Greg's face. "So . . . I hear you're Doctor DeMello's new partner."

Greg's smile was wry. "Good old Malino. No secrets here."

"*Au contraire, mon ami.*" Kim smiled with smug satisfaction. "I'll have you know we here in Malino have had two recent secrets. And massive ones, too."

His look of inquiry was enough to make her elaborate.

"Didn't you hear about Emma Lindsey and Matt Correa? It was such a big mystery, your mother must have mentioned it."

"Oh, yeah, the secret admirer thing."

Leave it to a man to take something unbelievably romantic and make it sound boring. The town had been mesmerized for over two months, wondering who was sending Emma beautiful flowers and signing them "from a secret admirer."

"And of course you have to know about Ben and Mele," she said, gesturing to the room at large. The happy couple were still standing, arms around one another, talking with well-wishers. "A lot of us were in on the Secret Santa thing. It took more than one person to arrange all those little surprises that led up to this evening."

"Secret Santa." Greg shook his head. "Amazing."

"You heard Ben explain that. Mele's nieces thought up the term. You know them, I'm sure, her brother Keola's kids? They're twins and they were doing Secret Santas at school. Didn't you ever do that?"

"Sure. In school. A long time ago."

Kim narrowed her eyes. Was he trying to say it was a practice suitable only for little kids?

"Adults do it too," she countered. "We have Secret Santas at the bank. We draw names right after Thanksgiving. That way no one feels they have to buy gifts for the whole staff."

"That makes sense." He nodded his approval. "Practical too."

"Is that all you're interested in? Practical? What about fun?"

"Fun is good. But practical is better."

Kim examined his face. He was dead serious. A glimmer of hope arose concerning a situation she'd been unhappily mulling over for weeks. It was at the back of her mind no matter what other activity she was involved in, gnawing at her. Could Greg have the answer?

"Can I ask you something?"

He looked leery but responded gamely, "Sure. Ask away."

Kim glanced nervously around the room. "It might take a while to explain. You want to come by the house and have some hot chocolate? That way I can explain," she ended.

Kim stopped speaking, chastising herself for her horrible presentation. He'd never agree. Would he? She sounded so dumb, repeating herself that way. She was flustered, and it was showing.

She watched him take another look around the big room. She glanced around as well, making note of the people who still milled about. Close friends of Mele and Ben lingered, of course, and the organizers of the party, Aunty Liliuokalani and Mr. Jardine, still wearing his red Santa shirt. The clean-up crew was busy gathering up the rubbish and stacking the tables.

Greg's gaze came back to rest on Kim, but she found herself unable to read anything into it.

"Sure, why not? Hot chocolate sounds good."

Relief flooded through her. This just might work.

She gave him her best smile and was flattered when he blinked in obvious confusion.

Chapter Two

Greg thought he must be nuts to have agreed to follow Kim home. He'd just barely moved back to town. And while his time in Honolulu had made him appreciate the charm of Malino, he didn't know if he was quite ready for the invasion of privacy that came with small-town living. Anyone on their way home from the party who saw his car at Kim's would jump to hasty conclusions. Word would spread. By Christmas morning the town would have them dating; by New Year's Eve they'd be practically engaged.

It was that thought—that certainty—that had Greg in his present situation.

He'd parked his truck in the usual place in his family's driveway. Kim's house wasn't very far away, especially if he cut through a few yards.

What he'd forgotten was that he hadn't done anything like this since his high school days. And attempting it so late in the evening had him stumbling through the dark to find his way to the Ascensions' kitchen door; he'd also forgotten a flashlight.

Kim still lived at home, of course. Unmarried young

adults did not live alone in Malino. There were no apartment buildings and few rooms to rent. Why would any young adult not related to anyone in town want to live there? There was very little business in Malino, except for farming and ranching, both difficult ways to make a living. Many of the young people, and even many of the older ones, commuted to service jobs at the luxury resorts on the Kohala coast. Young people lived with their parents until they married—and sometimes even afterward—unless their relatives had died and left them property, like Matt Correa and Ben Mendoza.

Greg had moved back into his old home when he finished his veterinary degree. It wasn't something he'd planned on doing. However, his father and grandmother had arrived in Honolulu for his graduation ceremony without his mother. She was too ill to travel, they informed him, but she had insisted he not be told until his exams were over.

So, with his mother ill with terminal cancer, he'd turned down the position he'd longed for in Honolulu and returned to Malino. It never occurred to him to look for his own place when his old room was available. And he knew his parents would have been hurt. In fact, the whole town would have been scandalized.

His mother had died late that summer. He'd only had two months with her, and once she was gone he was settled in with Doctor DeMello, too aware of the gratitude both the older doctor and the townspeople lavished on him to even consider moving back to Honolulu. It wasn't a bad deal, his partnership in the clinic. It just wasn't what he'd envisioned for himself.

It wasn't what his girlfriend, his almost-fiancée, had envisioned either. She was Honolulu-born and bred, and had apparently looked forward to life with an up-and-coming young veterinarian. She'd told him flat out that she would never live in a small town, showing little regret that it meant ending their year-long relationship. It was one more thing added to an emotional overload.

And there was his grandmother, who lived with them and was trying hard to cope with the death of her only child. She'd tended her daughter lovingly throughout her illness, remaining strong the whole time. Greg knew she was having a difficult time now. The strength that came so easily while her daughter was still alive had deserted her. His presence seemed to help. She enjoyed cooking his favorite dishes. If he wasn't careful, he'd weigh three hundred pounds by the end of next year. In addition, he was a good buffer between his father and his grandmother. The two of them had always had a prickly relationship, and with his mother gone it was sure to lead to eventual problems.

His mind still on his grandmother, Greg tripped over a low stone wall he'd forgotten was there. His grandmother had seemed happy these last few weeks. Or as happy as a woman whose only child had recently predeceased her could be. She'd thrown herself into the twin tasks of preparing for Christmas and fussing over him like he was a child of nine instead of a doctor of twenty-nine.

As he stopped to check that he was still heading the right way, he wondered what Kim could have to discuss with him. They'd been friends in high school but never boyfriend and girlfriend. She'd helped him with his writing assignments and he'd been too shy to ask her for a date. She'd been cute then, a perky, popular freshman, wide-eyed about high school and her close contact with a senior boy.

But now! She was beautiful now. Her facial features had matured past cuteness into classic beauty. She'd gained some height and her figure had matured. Cute had become *wow* and the teen's perkiness had become a lively appreciation for life.

Kim was waiting for him at the kitchen door, a grin making her look good enough to eat. It didn't hurt any that the house smelled like gingerbread, either. He'd always been partial to gingerbread.

Kim peered into the dark behind him. "Did you come through the yards from your house?"

"Of course."

She laughed. "Afraid to park outside in case everyone has us engaged by New Year's, huh?"

"New Year's? Are you kidding? They'd have me giving you a ring by Christmas night."

Kim laughed as she brought two mugs of fragrant hot chocolate to the table, then uncovered a round red container filled with gingersnaps.

"Gingerbread still your favorite?"

He smiled. "Yep. Can't believe you remember."

Before he had a chance to bite into the cookie he'd taken, she'd opened several more colorful containers. One held gingerbread hearts covered with a thin layer of pink icing. A larger one was home to whole families of gingerbread people—men with raisin buttons, women with icing skirts, little boys and little girls.

"Whoa," Greg said, stopping her from reaching for yet another container. "I think there's already enough here to feed the whole town."

Kim shrugged, looking sheepish. "I love to bake," she admitted.

"I didn't get a chance to tell you earlier," she said, putting the red container back on the counter. "I'm real sorry about your mother. I wanted to go to the funeral but I had to work . . ."

"That's okay." He cut off her apologies. "And thanks." For a little while, he would prefer to leave the painful memories behind and just enjoy the sight of a pretty girl, the taste of gingerbread, and the fond nostalgia for high school days.

He sipped his chocolate, grimacing when the hot liquid hit his mouth.

"That's hot," he said, stating the obvious.

He sucked in some air, then gave Kim a sad smile. He might prefer to push aside sad thoughts, but he felt bad at cutting off her expression of sympathy. He'd seen the surprise flash through her eyes. "I had a nice couple of months with her before she died."

Kim nodded sympathetically and took a tentative sip of her own chocolate. Finding the temperature manageable, she took another sip while trying to decide how best to approach her problem. She hardly expected a brilliant idea to jump out at her in the next thirty seconds. She'd had the ride home, and the time heating the milk and preparing the chocolate to come up with a solution. And the several months before that. Still, nothing wonderful had come to her.

Kim put down the mug and met Greg's eyes across the table. He'd always had a nice face and kind eyes. That hadn't changed; his eyes were still as kind as ever. It was so much easier to see them now without his thick glasses.

She swallowed, wishing for a bit of that courage he had noticed in Ben.

"I was hoping you might help me out with something," she began.

"If I can," Greg said immediately.

Kim was touched by his prompt reply. "You might not want to agree so quickly," she said with a grin. "At least wait to hear what it is."

"Okay," he agreed.

His expression was serious. Did he seem wary? She plunged ahead.

"You see," Kim began. "I'm in kind of a bind. Last year, I was dating a guy from Honokaa named Henry Leong. Things were pretty serious—at least I thought they were."

At just the thought of Henry, her breath seemed to catch in her throat, and she could feel a tic in her left cheek, just below her eye. Would Greg be able to see it? She'd never been able to determine if it was a noticeable phenomenon or just a figment of her imagination.

Resting her hand against the side of her face just in case, she went on.

"Then we were invited to a wedding in Waimea this past June."

She stopped, thinking that he probably wouldn't know—or care—about her life. But it was important to the current discussion.

"Did you know I lived in Hilo when I was in college?" she asked. "Six of us rented a house together. It was a lot cheaper than some of the alternatives. It had three bedrooms, so it was two to a room, which wasn't bad. But anyway," she shrugged at her babbling and continued. "One of my ex-roommates was the bride. She got married in June."

Greg nodded. "So you said."

"Oh, did I?" Kim was flustered, but she pushed on. "The rest of us were bridesmaids."

"All five of you?"

Kim was surprised. "Sure. Why not?"

Greg shrugged, but his discomfort with the subject was obvious. Why were guys so prickly about anything to do with weddings?

"It just seems like a lot."

Kim laughed. Men didn't have a clue.

"Not especially. Crystal was her maid of honor, and Stacey moved back to the mainland—to Seattle—and was just starting a new job and wasn't able to be there. So, actually, there were just three of us bridesmaids."

Greg seemed to find this a more acceptable number, and nodded his approval.

Kim tipped her face down so that she could see nothing but her mug and he could see nothing but the top of her head. She didn't want to see the inevitable look of pity on his face when she told him what had happened. It was the usual reaction to her story, and she hated it.

"To make a long and painful story short, while at this wedding, my dear Henry fell head over heels for one of my old roommates."

She raised her head and gave Greg a rueful smile. "Not the bride, fortunately."

"Well, I guess that was a good thing. For the couple and their guests both."

Greg smiled, and Kim looked carefully into his face. There was no pity there, thank goodness. Sympathy, maybe. Kindness, definitely.

Kim felt better. This might work after all. She grinned. "Well, she was the maid of honor, so it got a little odd when she wasn't there for the throwing of the bouquet. That's when we all realized she was gone."

"She was the maid of honor?" Greg said with a chuckle. "Ironic, huh?"

Kim laughed, but there was little mirth in it. "Maid of honor. Yeah. With no honor."

She tried to take another sip of her chocolate and was surprised to find the cup empty. She stood and moved over to the stove to refill her mug.

"How's your chocolate, Greg? Would you like more?"

"Sure. It's good. I haven't had hot chocolate since I was a kid. Mom always called it cocoa."

He stared blankly down at his mug, and Kim wasn't sure what to say. She settled for the obvious. "I'm glad you're enjoying it."

After refilling their cups, Kim sat back down beside him.

"To pick up where I left off . . . my boyfriend and my old roommate disappeared together from the reception before the cake was even cut. It was apparently one of those Hollywood things—you know, where their eyes met across the room and they knew immediately that they were meant for each other."

"Geez."

Kim looked up at his softly voiced comment and smiled.

"Thanks. It was embarrassing. Her date and I were left wondering what had happened to our escorts. It's a good thing I'd driven myself over. Otherwise I would have had to beg for a ride home and that would have been even worse."

Greg was shaking his head in disbelief, and Kim smiled. He was still the nice guy she remembered from high school, despite his new hunky looks. Some good-looking guys could be real jerks. She was glad that Greg wasn't one of those. Maybe there was hope for her after all.

"Anyway, when she called me afterward I told her it was no big deal, that we were heading for the end anyway."

Greg offered a wry grin. "Lying through your teeth, weren't you?"

There was sympathy in his voice, but she could detect no pity in his expression. In fact, he seemed like he approved.

She shrugged. "I didn't want her to know how hurt and angry I was. At him. At her."

"I'm surprised she called you."

"She said she didn't want it to ruin our beautiful friendship."

His reaction was a quick exhalation of breath that sounded suspiciously like a snort.

"You're kidding."

"Nope. Those were her exact words."

They stared at each other for a moment, wondering at the impertinence.

"And . . . ?" he prompted.

"Well, then she called a few weeks later and invited me to be in the wedding."

"They invited you to their wedding?"

Kim nodded. "Not only to be a guest, but to be a bridesmaid. Just like we'd promised each other." She sighed as Greg, again shook his head in disbelief. "I guess I did too good a job of pretending I didn't care about losing Henry."

Greg's voice softened. "Are you still in love with him?"

"Are you kidding?" Kim answered instantly.

Her voice rose with indignation, and she had to make an effort to lower it. Her mother had gone straight to bed when they'd gotten home, and she didn't want to wake her.

"I thank God every day for letting me find out about him before we actually got engaged. Imagine if we'd been getting married and he'd fallen for Crystal. She would have been part of my bridal party, after all. If it was really inevitable . . ." Her voice trailed off as she futilely waved a hand before her.

Greg reached out and took hold of her hand, covering it with both of his. Kim swallowed at the warmth that extended far beyond the hand he'd enveloped so tenderly with his. She'd heard that he was an excellent vet. It must be this compassion that endeared him to animals. And that gentle touch she was experiencing.

With real regret, she watched him take his hands away

after a few seconds. But the warmth remained, as did the comfort that had come with it.

"So what do you want me to do?" He seemed genuinely puzzled.

Kim bit her lip. This was the hard part. She hated asking favors. Yet here she was, getting ready to ask this almost-stranger to do something very special for her.

"Well . . ." She peered up at Greg through her eyelashes, wondering if the bashful look would help. "Crystal made this big apology when we got together to order our dresses. And I not only told her it didn't matter, I kind of indicated that I had this wonderful new boyfriend . . ."

"Uh-oh."

Greg's lips drew downward and the motion made Kim's stomach tumble in the same direction.

"I think I'm beginning to see where this is headed," Greg said. He didn't look happy.

"I wouldn't tell her who it was, of course, because . . ."

". . . there wasn't actually anyone to name," he finished for her.

She nodded glumly.

"But won't she know that we haven't been dating?"

Kim shook her head. "I don't think so. She's not from Malino, remember, and neither is Henry."

A glimmer of hope shimmered in her eyes, and Greg knew he was lost. She looked so encouraged that his heart did a back flip. How could he crush her dreams, even if it would cause major gossip along the Malino grapevine?

Then a thought flashed through his mind—suddenly, out of nowhere. Major gossip about the two of them might not be a bad thing. It could even work to his advantage. He began to grin. If the townspeople thought he and Kim were an item, all the local matchmakers would leave him alone. There had been a grace period right after his mother's death, but since Halloween, he'd heard about numerous nieces, granddaughters and cousins, all most anxious to meet him.

Yep, that alone would make it worthwhile. And he'd be able to help his old friend too.

"Okay. I'll do it."

Kim flew up out of her chair, throwing her arms around him. A comforting warmth flooded his body and he was sorry when she let him go.

"Thank you, thank you! You're a lifesaver!"

She started to lower herself back into her chair. But then, too excited to sit, she began to pace—from the table to the counter, then over to the sink, eventually completing a circle around the room. Greg recalled that she had been the same way in high school, rarely able to stay still for long. Her energy was one of the things he'd liked about her.

"You don't know how worried I've been," Kim admitted. "I told her I'd be bringing you. I mean, that I'd bring him, the new boyfriend. Not that you're my new boyfriend."

Greg raised a hand, palm outward, even though he liked the way her cheeks were turning pink as she tried to explain their convoluted new relationship. "It's okay. I know what you meant."

"I just didn't know what I was going to do. I'd pretty much run out of possibilities."

The words tripped from her mouth, one after another, almost too quickly to comprehend. But he managed to follow the gist of it without trouble as she ran through all the men she'd considered, then eliminated for whatever reason.

It was coming back to him now, her stream-of-consciousness dialogue, the way she rarely stood still. She hadn't changed much, except in appearance.

As Kim came back around the table, she hugged him

again. Once more, warmth flooded his body. His heart rate tripled, and he found his arms itching to encircle her slim form and pull her tight against him.

Greg decided it had been way too long since he'd been out on a date. How could a mere hug affect him like this?

"Oh, I can't thank you enough," Kim gushed. "You've saved my life."

Still pondering his reaction to her, Greg sought to distract himself. He pulled back from her as much as the back of his chair allowed.

"So . . . when is this wedding?"

Kim had resumed her pacing, and her words came from the other side of the room.

"Valentine's Day."

That distracted him from thoughts of her physical closeness all right.

Valentine's Day. Well, that would get the old gossips going. Yep, he wouldn't have to worry about any matchmakers once word got out about that. And word would get out, he was sure of it.

He noticed that Kim had stopped pacing and was watching him. She seemed concerned, perhaps due to his grim expression. He worked to smooth his facial features into something resembling a smile.

"Valentine's Day, huh? Okay." He took a deep breath. "Sure." This was going to work out well. He'd mention it to his grandmother in the morning and the whole town would know by dinnertime. Guaranteed. Violet Moniz was a major supporting limb of the Malino grapevine.

He could see the relief spreading over Kim's face. That, at least, made him feel better. It was the season for giving, and he would be giving an old friend a gift she desperately wanted. And it was only one night. He'd even get a gift in return—temporary relief from the town's famous matchmakers. One night in return for two months of bachelor comfort. He barely felt guilty about that at all.

When he tuned back in, he realized Kim was telling him about the wedding.

"It's going to be at the Pua Lani Gardens in Hilo and they'll have fireworks and everything. It's going to be a huge affair."

Kim winced at her poor choice of words, and Greg reached for her hand. She'd stopped pacing and resumed her seat beside him.

"I just hope you won't feel lost there," Kim continued. "I don't know how she'll arrange the seating, but if there's a big head table, you might have to sit alone."

Greg was suddenly lost. Why wouldn't he sit with his date?

"Wait a minute. I thought you and I were going together."

"Yes, we are. But I'm a bridesmaid, remember, so I might not be able to sit with you."

He shook his head at the whole business. The girl steals her boyfriend, then continues to claim friendship and even asks her to be a bridesmaid. And she actually accepts. It was more than he would have done. He'd never understand women's thought processes.

"You don't find this situation a little strange?" he asked.

Kim's eyebrows flew up.

"Strange? Of course it's strange." Her arms shot upward and it took effort not to shout her outrage. "It's beyond strange. But what can I do? We agreed years ago that we would have all the roommates as bridesmaids when we got married. So far, everyone has."

Kim worked to bring her breathing under control so that she could speak calmly as she tried to make him understand.

"I was so hurt that Henry could just leave like that. I thought we'd be getting married one day, and he took one look at Crystal and no longer loved me. But I decided I could either go to my room and cry for the next six months, or keep my pride and pretend I didn't care."

Kim set her shoulders back and firmed her chin. "My mother thinks I should have told Crystal to forget it and terminate the friendship. Crystal always did try to best me in everything." She turned back to Greg. "She was a business major too, but in merchandising. I think she resented the fact that I always got better grades than she did. Though I did study harder," she added with a grin. "Crystal liked to party."

"Then you deserved your good grades."

Kim acknowledged his words, but it didn't settle her restlessness. She opened and closed a cupboard without removing anything, then turned to face Greg once again.

"I guess that's part of it, that old competitiveness. I just refuse to let her win. And if I said I wouldn't be in the wedding party, or showed up without a date, then she wins. She might not gloat, but she would spend a lot of time telling the others how awful it was that her falling in love killed our friendship." She wrinkled her nose at him. "Of course, they would know the whole story and could make their own judgments. But then I'd feel as if I was compelling them to chose sides."

She raised her shoulders almost to her ears before letting them drop in a dramatic, exaggerated shrug. "This whole situation is absolutely ridiculous. And I can't help thinking it was mostly Henry's fault. He took one look at her and that was it; he decided she was the one, and he had to have her. Knowing him as well as I do, I can totally believe that happened—or at least, Henry believed that it did. And she was so dazzled by his attitude, she fell too. Can you blame her? It is awfully romantic."

There was that word again—*romantic*. Greg was hearing it often tonight.

Noting the wistful tone of Kim's final sentence, Greg examined carefully her face. When he spoke, his voice was gentle and very quiet.

"You aren't still in love with him, are you?"

She'd been looking out the darkened window, but she spun back around to face him. "Of course not."

Her reply was so quick, he wondered if she even knew the truth. He'd believed her the first time she'd answered this question for him, but now he wasn't quite as convinced.

But he did know that he would help her out.

"Then we'll go to the party, we'll dance and watch the fireworks, and have such a good time everyone will be envious."

Kim smiled, her mouth beginning to open. He rushed to speak before she could.

"And you don't have to thank me again. That's what friends are for."

"Still . . ."

Kim leaned forward and placed a soft kiss on his cheek.

"Thank you, Greg. You're the best friend a girl ever had."

Greg breathed in slowly, wondering if he was getting any oxygen or if it was all being sucked out of the air by Kim's proximity. He needed to get out of here. The walk home would be dark, but it was just what he needed right now. There would be plenty of fresh air. It would clear his head and give him time to think.

As Kim backed away from him, he brushed his hair off his forehead and stood.

"Well, thanks for the cocoa, ah, the hot chocolate, Kim. And the cookies. I felt eighteen again."

Kim smiled warily. "I hope that's a good thing."

"Yep." Greg moved toward the door. He kept his voice low so as not to awaken anyone in the house. "Eighteen was a good year."

He brushed the back of his hand lightly down the side of her face.

"I'll see you soon, then."

"Goodnight, Greg. And thanks again."

Greg could hear the sweetness of her voice for minutes afterward as he struggled to make his way through the yards. He should have waited for his eyes to adjust to the darkness, but he was in too much of a hurry to get away. He needed distance from Kim, and he needed it quickly. He welcomed the cool, humid night air, the thickening mist that dampened his hair and shirt.

What were these strange feelings he was having all of a sudden? He'd obviously been caught up in his losses, his work, and his family for too long a time. A simple thank-you kiss—an almost sisterly kiss—should not have aroused the kind of feelings that had overwhelmed him.

Greg tripped over the same stone wall he'd bruised himself against on his walk to Kim's house. Muttering under his breath, he stopped long enough to massage his aching ankle—the other ankle. He'd have a matched set of bruises.

As he let himself into his own house, Greg saw again the hope and the happiness that had danced through Kim's eyes when he agreed to her proposition. She was so pretty when she was happy.

Well, she was pretty anyway, but her beauty increased with the delight radiating from her eyes. She had such beautiful eyes, they sparkled when she smiled. If the eyes were truly a reflection of the soul, then Kim had a forgiving, happy soul.

With a firm shake of his head, Greg threw off his strange, philosophical thoughts. Where on earth had they come from? It was bad enough how flustered he'd gotten when he held her—even in the most innocent of hugs. Not to mention what her lips had done to him. They were so soft . . . so sweet . . .

"Greg, is that you?"

The low-pitched voice came from the room just beyond the bathroom, startling Greg out of his daydreams.

Greg sighed. The joys of living at home. It was hard on a young man who'd been on his own for several years.

"Yep, Dad. It's me. Sorry if I woke you."

"No, no. Just settling in." His father's stooped figure moved into the doorway of his bedroom. "Hard to sleep when you get old."

He looked down the hall at Greg, still in his outside jacket.

"Nice party tonight. Nothing like it before, that's for sure."

Greg had to agree. "That Ben sure has a lot of courage, proposing in front of the whole town that way." Greg shook his head in wonder.

Frank stepped out into the hall.

"Oh, that didn't take a whole lot of courage, son. It was love that made him do it. He knew she wouldn't be able to resist such a romantic gesture."

Greg frowned. There was that word again. Romantic.

Would he ever love like that? For a while, he'd thought he'd had that kind of love with Teri. When he'd discovered that material things were more important to her than his love, he'd become bitter and disillusioned. Love scared the living daylights out of him. To love that way again, exposing himself for more hurt. To love like his father had loved his mother.

Greg looked at his father, at the frail figure he'd become. He'd aged ten years in the past few months. So had his grandmother. Greg didn't think his own physical appearance had changed, but he knew that he was different, too. He'd loved his mother and it had hurt like the devil to lose her. How did you cope with loving someone so deeply when you knew you might lose them at any time? His father had been a strong, upright man before his wife's death. Now he seemed so old, his back perpetually rounded. He barely seemed to sleep anymore. Greg missed the reassuring sound of his father's snores, even though he'd complained about the noise his whole life.

Greg put his hand on his father's shoulder and squeezed.

"Better try to get some sleep, Dad. Sorry if I woke you by coming in so late."

"No, no problem, son."

Greg left his father standing in the hallway as he entered his own room and closed the door. The question of love and whether it was worth the risk was more than he could reconcile this evening. It likely was more than he could ever come to understand, even if he spent the rest of his life on the problem. For now, he'd be happy to spend some time with Kim, enjoy her company, and not have to worry about trying to avoid the inevitable fix-ups of well-meaning neighbors. His heart was still bruised from Teri's harsh treatment; he'd protect it as best he could.

Chapter Three

If he'd thought about it before climbing into bed the previous evening, Greg would have assumed he would have had trouble falling asleep. There was the late night, the town party where he'd seen so many old friends again—many of whom he hadn't seen since the funeral. Then the meeting with Kim, and her story about the roommate from hell and the wedding on Valentine's Day.

He didn't know if anyone had seen him at Kim's house, but in a small town, secrets were hard to keep. One of Kim's neighbors could have seen into the lighted kitchen; someone might even have watched him make his way through the yards. The assumptions he knew the town would be making should have kept him awake all night. Not to mention the way Kim could make him forget his resolve not to lose his heart again.

Despite the apparent distractions, Greg awoke at eight from a deep, refreshing sleep. No dreams had disturbed his night, and he might have slept on if not for the neighbor's noisy dog. Mumbling about people who couldn't keep their pets quiet, he caught sight of the clock and revised his mutterings.

Thank God for noisy animals. Nature's alarm clock. And what had happened to his man-made alarm clock, he wondered.

He rushed into the bathroom to shower and brush his teeth. Shaving could wait. The animals wouldn't care if he had stubble on his chin.

By the time he arrived in the kitchen, Greg's mood had improved. The sun was shining, bringing its warmth to the island. Birds were singing, and the dog had finally stopped barking. He could smell not only fresh coffee, but frying Spam.

"Good morning, Vovo." Greg bent to kiss his grandmother's cheek. Although she would be seventy-five in January, Violet's cheek was as soft and smooth as any twenty-year-old's. There were spiderwebs of wrinkles around her eyes, and her neck and arms were not as firm as they had been, but her complexion was the envy of many a younger woman.

"Got in late last night."

There was a teasing quality to her voice that made Greg feel young. Sometimes he resented it, but this morning he just smiled. He did feel young this morning. He would never see eighteen again, but pleasure could be found in the memories.

"I stopped by to see Kim Ascension after the party. We went to school together," he reminded her. Not that he needed to. Her mind was as sharp as ever. "She made hot chocolate, and we visited."

Violet nodded. "Nice girl. Works at the bank."

Greg poured some coffee into a large mug, and sat down. Violet brought over a plate of eggs with toast and fried Spam.

He accepted the plate with a smile. "You're going to

make me fat, Vovo. I haven't eaten like this since I was a growing boy. I'll have to hit the road for some jogging."

She dismissed his concern. "Your grandpa, rest his soul, ate like this every day and he was healthy his whole life, till the day he died."

Greg hid the smile that was his reaction to her rather interesting logic.

She poured herself another cup of coffee and sat down. The paper was on the table, folded open at the drugstore ad, but she ignored it.

"So what did you and Kim talk about?" Violet asked bluntly.

His mouth full, Greg shrugged a vague reply. Swallowing, he took a sip of coffee, then attempted an answer.

"We talked about old times. And she asked a favor."

"You haven't seen her in years and she asks a favor?" She was insulted for him.

Greg smiled again, openly this time. "Don't worry, you're going to like this one. I think."

He took another mouthful of food, letting her wait to hear what the favor was and why she would like it. But he already felt that she approved of Kim, so he was sure she would endorse the upcoming date. And spread the word.

"She's invited to a wedding on Valentine's Day. Or rather . . . she's *in* a wedding on Valentine's Day. And she needed a date. It was kind of a complicated story."

"Oh, you mean that woman who stole her boyfriend." Violet nodded. "I didn't know the wedding was on Valentine's Day."

Greg realized he should have known that no explanations would be necessary. The old small-town network was as efficient as ever.

"So are you going with her?" Violet asked.

Greg caught a speculative gleam in his grandmother's eye as she gazed calmly across the table. Just as he'd suspected, word would be all over Malino by sunset. He had to fight hard to hide a satisfied smile. His grandmother had been urging him to date again for some time. He'd been too cynical of women's motivations to even think about it, but renewing his friendship with Kim might be just the thing to help resolve his mixed feelings about the fairer sex. At least there was no question of romantic dating; this was a practical setup that had advantages for both sides.

"Yep. I remember Kim from high school, though I was too shy to ask her out back then. She was younger, and popular too." He shook his head at his teenage insecurities, though they weren't too different from his adult ones—at least where women were concerned. "I always liked her, and she doesn't seem to have changed."

Violet nodded her agreement. "I like Kim. She's a good bank teller too, never makes mistakes."

Greg grinned. "That's a good thing in a bank teller."

"She didn't deserve treatment like that from that boyfriend of hers," Violet continued. "Paula told me all about what he did. Took her to a wedding and just left her there. Took off with one of the other bridesmaids." Her voice was suitably indignant.

"It was the maid of honor," he corrected with a grin. "Get it? The maid of honor?"

Violet, however, didn't crack a smile. It wasn't really that funny. It was more of a pun, the kind of thing that made people roll their eyes and groan. At least she hadn't done that. And Kim hadn't the night before, he realized. This friendship of theirs just might work out.

Greg took another bite of his toast, following up with a sip of coffee. "I was amazed that she would even go to this girl's wedding, much less be part of the wedding party."

"Oh, I'm sure she'll hold her head up and pretend it doesn't matter. Kim has pride," Violet said, approval apparent in her voice. "But her poor heart almost broke at the time."

Greg nodded. He'd wondered just how bad she'd felt back in June. Now, six months later, she was mostly mad—both at Henry and at Crystal. But Vovo was probably right; back in June she must have been heartbroken.

His hand stopped, his fork halfway to his mouth, as he wondered whether she truly was over it. Was her anger just a cover for a heart still aching for Henry?

"She says she's not sorry it happened," he ventured. He wanted to see Vovo's reaction.

"Well, sure. What else could she say?" Violet added more sugar to her coffee and stirred it thoughtfully. "But Paula did say Kim was relieved it happened before they got married."

"Married?" Greg's head came up in surprise. "She said they weren't even engaged."

"They weren't," his grandmother agreed. "But everybody knew they would be."

Greg finished up his meal as he took in this information. So it was a serious thing, that relationship that had ended so suddenly on what should have been a happy day for Kim and her friends. Kim had said that she'd seen herself spending the rest of her life with Henry, but he'd thought it mostly daydreams. But his grandmother apparently thought it had been a very serious relationship. Poor Kim. It was such a public way to have her almost-fiancé leave. No matter what she said, she probably was still getting over it.

Greg emptied his coffee cup with a final sip and a soft sigh. Kim was determined to attend the wedding because she wanted to show Henry and Crystal—especially Henry—

that she could manage quite well without them, thank you very much. And that very attitude told him that she still cared deeply about old Henry.

Greg wondered just how stressed out she would be by the time the wedding actually arrived. She'd already been living with the prospect of it, not to mention worrying over finding a date for almost six months. No wonder she'd spent so much of the previous night pacing restlessly around the kitchen. She probably needed that physical activity for stress release. Maybe he should invite her to play tennis to use up some of that energy she was keeping pent-up inside.

Greg was surprised by the thought, and even more so by the pleasure that came along with the idea of spending more time with Kim. Perhaps Kim and her problems were just the thing he needed to stop his mind from dwelling on the losses he'd suffered in the past year. His busy practice was distracting, but he faced the long nights alone. He hadn't managed to pick up any old friendships; most of his old friends who were still around were already married, with young families that took up their time and attention. He felt sure he and Kim would be good for each other.

After depositing his plate in the sink, Greg returned to the table to give his grandmother a kiss on the top of her head. When had her hair gotten so thin? He could see her scalp, pink as a newborn's, between the slicked-back strands of white.

"Goodbye, Vovo. Have a good day. I still have shopping to do today, so I'll let you know if I'll make it home for dinner, okay?"

"Do try to make it home, dear. I'm going to make oxtail soup for tonight. Remember how your mother always made it just before Christmas?"

"Yes, I remember." He rested his head against the old

lady's, offering the comfort of his embrace. "I'll try to be here."

"If not, I'll keep some warm in the oven," she said.

Greg's pleasant memories of Kim flew into the atmosphere as sadness once again gained the upperhand in his life. Christmas had always been his mother's favorite time of year, and she'd filled it with yearly traditions. They were trying hard to spend the season in her usual all-out celebratory manner. But it just wasn't the same. It might have been different if Teri had been here beside him. But the thought of her fickleness just made it worse. *You couldn't count on love.* It always managed to kick you in the gut, whether it was the loyal familial type or romantic love. Better to just try to avoid it altogether.

Kim fingered a wool cardigan, wondering if her mother really needed another sweater. Still, Christmas was just two days away and she had yet to decide on a gift for her closest relative. Why were mothers so darned difficult to buy for?

"Hey, Kim. How's it going?"

She turned at the greeting, unable to contain the wide smile that came unbidden at the sight of Greg Yamamoto.

"Well, hi. I'm great. How about you?"

Her eyes skimmed over his athletic form. He wore faded jeans, a bit grubby around the knees, but soft and touchable and molded to his muscles. Obviously, he was in great shape.

Once again she wondered what had happened to the nerdy young man she'd known in high school. He must have gotten seriously into fitness once he started college. And it was amazing what the lack of glasses could do for a man's face. The dark stubble on his chin this evening added a lot to his appeal as well.

"So you're not done with your shopping yet, either, huh?" His glance went from her face to the sweater in her hands and back again.

She nodded. "You too?"

"Yep. Got my dad some new tools, but Vovo is real hard. Got any ideas?"

Kim had to laugh. "I doubt if I'll be any help. I'm still trying to find something for my mom." She sighed. "Parents—and grandparents," she added with a nod toward him, "are so hard to buy for. I can always find something for my sister, and her kids are easy too. They mostly tell me right out what they want," she added, and Greg joined her in a short moment of laughter. "But with parents, for the most part, they already have everything they want. So it's really hard."

Greg looked at the sweater still in her hands. "Think Vovo might like a sweater?"

Kim frowned as she examined the sweater once again. "I don't know. Most women can use another sweater, what with all the cool damp weather we get. And I like this color." She ran her fingers over the wool, a soft blue several shades lighter than denim. "It just seems so impersonal, you know?"

Greg's expression seemed puzzled, but he nodded agreeably anyway.

Kim replaced the sweater on the table in front of her.

"Does Vovo have any hobbies?" she asked, as she moved to a rack beside the table of sweaters and began browsing through hangers of blouses.

"That's an idea. Let me think . . ."

Kim's mouth began to tip upward as amusement lightened her mood. He had to think about whether or not his grandmother had a hobby? A grandmother who lived in the same house?

With a frustrated sigh, she stopped sorting through the blouses. Nothing looked appealing, except the guy who was trying to remember what his grandmother did in her spare time.

"Hmm, she sews. She does this embroidery stuff, bright colored flowers, mostly."

"Oh, that's right." Kim smiled brightly at Greg. She should have remembered that. "She does Japanese-style embroidery. I've seen it. She does gorgeous work." She smiled brightly at Greg. "There's your answer then. You can get her an assortment of threads. Embroiderers can always use more thread."

Greg, instead of looking happy at this wonderful plan, looked more distressed than ever. Panicked, even.

"Thread? Where on earth do I get that?"

Kim felt better. It wasn't that he didn't like her idea, just that he didn't know how to follow up. Really, he looked like someone had asked him to produce a slice of green cheese from the moon.

"Don't worry, I know where to get it."

Greg looked better at that, but solving his problem didn't help her own dilemma.

"I don't suppose you have any ideas for my mom?" she asked teasingly.

Greg assumed a serious expression as he considered this. He even rubbed his fingers along the side of his face while he thought. Kim watched his strong fingers rub against the dark stubble and felt a shiver all along her arms. She was glad when he brought his hand back down to his side.

"Does she have any hobbies?"

Kim almost snorted in disbelief. "Oh, come on. That was my line. Don't you think I've thought of that?"

"And?"

"And what? She used to embroider, too, but she hasn't

done much of that stuff the past few years. I know she still has lots of thread and embroidery supplies. Since Dad died, she's so busy with the house and yard she doesn't have time for much of anything. She still works full-time at the medical center, you know."

His expression didn't waver. In fact, one side of his lips began to tip upward in the beginnings of a smile. "That's it."

Kim still didn't get it. "*What's* it?"

"Working around the house and yard is her hobby now." He stated it with matter-of-fact finality.

Kim thought this over. "Okay. Maybe."

"I've seen your mom outside working in the yard. She likes it, Kim. I'm sure of it. Does she act like she does it just to get it done? Is it a burden? Or does she go out there and kind of relax, enjoy the act of beautifying the yard, growing flowers?"

Kim reflected for a moment. Five years ago, right after her father had died after being hit by a drunk driver, her mother had assumed the yardwork as an extra burden. But as time passed, Kim realized that she devoted more and more of her time to it. It was no longer just mowing the grass and trimming the shrubbery. She spent a lot of time outdoors, planting and replanting flowers, trimming trees and shrubs into pleasing shapes, pulling weeds. Raking even, a task that Kim considered nothing but a waste of time.

"You know, I think you have something there," she told Greg. "But how does that help me find her a Christmas present?"

"There has to be something she'd like that would help her in her work. Just like my father with tools. He's got lots of them, but he always enjoys getting more."

"Hmm." Kim thought this over. She only knew about the

basics of gardening tools. Hoes, shovels, trowels . . . those things she could identify, but she was sure they already had them all.

"I don't know a whole lot about gardening equipment, Greg. And I also don't really know exactly what we have."

Greg took her arm and began to hurry her out of the store.

"Come along, then. We'll just have to do a B and E to find out."

"A *B and E?*"

"You know . . ." He grinned at her, lifting his eyebrow in a slightly mocking manner. Then he leaned in close to her ear before lowering his voice and whispering. "Breaking and entering."

Kim laughed. She didn't even attempt to keep her voice lowered. "Someone's been watching too many cop shows on TV."

He sobered. "Mom loved cop shows on TV. We watched a lot of television together when she got too weak to do much. Those old *Hawaii Five-O* shows were her favorite."

Kim grasped his hand, squeezing it lightly.

He accepted the gesture without comment, but Kim was certain he appreciated it.

"Come on . . ." His voice was quieter, but he seemed no less enthusiastic. "Shall we take my car or yours?"

In no time at all, Kim found herself skulking through the yards behind her home, stealthily winding her way from Greg's house toward her own.

The absurdity of the situation finally hit her, and she stifled something that sounded embarrassingly like a giggle.

Greg stopped long enough to look back. "Did you say something?"

"No."

Still, it was funny, the two of them—two respectfully employed grown-ups—sneaking around through yards on their way to break into her own garage.

Not that they needed to break in. It was her house, after all, and she knew where the key was kept. So they weren't doing anything illegal.

Well, it wasn't really *her* house, she thought, sobering somewhat at the thought of illegalities. But it was the home where she'd lived her entire life. And while she didn't do much in the yard except for picking flowers and pulling a few weeds, she knew where her mother kept all the gardening stuff. Right there in a large cupboard in the carport. And the key was hanging off a nail right around the corner, under the roof overhang.

Just in time, Greg warned her about a low stone wall at the back of the Stevens' property. She probably would have tripped over it and fallen flat on her face.

"Banged my ankles against that last night," he grumbled.

"Thanks," Kim murmured.

It wasn't completely dark out, but the sun was going down and things were looking shadowy and gray. Greg must have gone straight to the store in Kamuela after work, just as she had done. In fact, Kim felt sure her mother was expecting her home for dinner any time now. How would she feel if she knew her younger daughter was presently sneaking into the carport?

It was a standard design for a carport: at the far end, there were two wide folding-style closet doors. The first set hid the washing machine, with room for a dryer, though they didn't have one. Took too much electricity, her father had always said. A few clotheslines strung across the carport served as their natural drying system. In fact, there were some towels hanging there now, helping to hide Kim and Greg.

At the other side of the carport there was another set of doors. These hid a large storage space, large enough for the lawnmower and whatever else was needed to keep up the yard. Kim had never seen the appeal of playing in the dirt, so she had no idea what lay behind the doors, other than the lawnmower. It had been years since she'd been in there.

It was dim in the carport, with only a little light from a bulb beside the door that her mother left on when Kim was out. As she fitted the key into the padlock, she whispered a question to Greg.

"Are you sure you'll know what everything is for, and what she might need?"

Kim needed some reassurance. She felt so silly about creeping around this way that she needed to know this was not an exercise in futility.

"Sure I'll know. I can take care of yards, you know."

Greg sounded offended at her lack of trust.

"Mr. Macho," she muttered, still fumbling with the key. But she knew he'd heard her when she saw him smile.

"No, I just had to do it when I was in high school. My job, you know. I'm sure you had them too."

"Of course. Household chores." Every child in Malino had had household chores—at least back when they were children. She wasn't so sure about the current generation. "But I cleaned the house."

"Girl jobs, huh? I bet your brother did the outside stuff."

"Yep. He would have taken over after Dad died if he hadn't been on the mainland."

The lock lay in her hand now, and she whispered a warning.

"Try to be careful. The door creaks, I think. It's been a while since I was in here."

But the door did not creak. It slid open soundlessly, the

accordion-like sections sliding together smoothly on the overhead runners.

"Good thing I brought this."

Greg turned on the flashlight he'd thought to bring along, shining it into the dark closet. The lawnmower sat in isolated splendor in the space to the right. To the left, hoe, shovel, and rake stood against the back wall beneath shelves holding fertilizer, bug and weed spray, and small tools like trowels and pruning shears.

"Wow." Kim spoke softly, but her voice showed that she was impressed by what she saw. "This is all so neat and organized."

"It is," Greg agreed. "Okay, I've seen enough. Let's go before one of the neighbors calls the cops on us."

"Oh, my gosh, I never even thought of that." Kim fumbled with the door and the lock as she hurried to comply with his request. "Mrs. Arruda is always looking over here. At least during the daytime. Let's hope she's busy watching TV tonight."

Greg's voice was low and reassuring. "I'm sure she's busy with the news or *Wheel of Fortune*. Vovo never misses *Wheel of Fortune*."

Kim gave a huge sigh of relief as she finally snapped the padlock shut.

As soon as they got back to Greg's truck parked in his driveway, they both collapsed against it, laughing. Leaning against one another, they relived the scare they'd gotten. As they were returning the key to its hidden nail, they'd both heard a door open close by. Without waiting to see what was happening, they'd both run for the backyard. Stumbling in the now complete dark, they didn't even take time to turn on Greg's flashlight. They were already laughing as they made it to the driveway at Greg's.

"It must have been Mrs. Arruda," Kim insisted. "Oh, dear, almost caught breaking into my own house."

"Probably just letting out the dog," Greg said, though he was laughing too.

"She doesn't have a dog."

"The cat, then."

"No cat either."

Greg leaned over, trying to get his breath back after their mad dash. Kim was doing the same, holding onto a stitch in her side.

"Do you think she called the cops?" Kim finally managed. Her sides hurt from laughing, but it felt good. It felt even better when Greg put his arm around her. She knew he was just trying to keep her from collapsing completely, but it was very nice to have someone like him care.

"Hard to tell. You can't trust someone who doesn't have a pet."

As his hand tightened on her shoulder and warmth raced through her, she felt the laughter flee. It was replaced by a serious pull of attraction. She wondered if Greg could possibly be feeling it too. For as soon as she'd identified the pleasant feeling seeping through her, she felt him stiffen, then pull away.

Suddenly she was no longer consumed with fun and laughter. In fact, she'd been thrown into the opposite extreme. Post-traumatic stress, she assumed—the stress of sneaking around, of Greg's closeness, by the thought that a busybody neighbor might have seen the flashlight and called the cops.

Good grief, the cops! She pushed even farther away from Greg. How did she ever let him talk her into this? How could she ever explain that she was breaking into her own closet? Her cousin Lono might answer the call, and she'd never hear the end of it. And her mother would hear.

Suddenly, she felt as though a flock of butterflies had taken up residence in her stomach.

"Are you all right?" Greg's voice was full of concern.

"I'm fine." But thoughts of what might have happened made her knees weak, and she wondered if she'd have fallen flat on her face if Greg hadn't grabbed her arms and held her up.

Now that the sneaking part was over, Kim was sure those bones in her knees would reappear any moment and support her weight as they were meant to.

If only Greg would move away, maybe she could get back her equilibrium and things would return to normal.

They stood for a moment, breathing quietly, lost in their individual thoughts. When Kim finally felt ready to look over at Greg, she was startled to see that his face was pale and grim.

"What?" she asked, her voice edged with panic. Had he seen a police car? "What's wrong?"

"Nothing."

But his voice was tight with control, and his complexion remained pale. Perhaps it was just an illusion created by the strange light from the strings of colored bulbs that edged the eaves, but she didn't think so.

"Something's wrong," Kim stated firmly, in a tone that demanded an answer.

Greg didn't glance at her. He continued to gaze at the house, at the strings of colored lights and the decorated tree that stood inside, visible through the front windows. A thick wreath hung on the front door.

"Mother loved Christmas."

Kim felt a tightness in her chest, as though a wide band had encircled her heart and pulled itself tight.

"We didn't want to change how we celebrate. For her."

Kim could barely hear Greg as he continued to speak,

but sound traveled in the night and she felt certain he didn't want everyone in Malino to hear him. Or maybe it was just the people inside that he didn't want overhearing.

Kim had to clear her throat. Darn nighttime air. The dampness made her throat constrict.

"She'll be noticing," Kim assured him. "And enjoying it every bit as much as she always did."

Greg nodded. Then he purposely turned away from the house with all its Christmas cheer and looked directly into Kim's face.

"Come on," he said, opening the passenger-side door of his truck and gesturing her in. "We can still get over to Young's General Store before they close and get your mother's gift."

After helping her climb into the high seat, he hurried around to the driver's side and got in.

"Where do we go for mine?"

Kim felt bad, but there was no getting around it. "We can't get it tonight. You'll have to go to the needlework store over in Kamuela, and it won't be open this late. I'll tell you where and all, though, and you can go tomorrow."

He frowned. "I have to work. It's Christmas Eve, too."

"You can get it on your lunch hour. In fact, I'll call Lydia in the morning and tell her what you need, and you can just run in and pick it up. Unless you want to call her yourself? She might even wrap it for you."

"Would you do that for me? Call her and all?"

He smiled and her heart skipped a beat. How had the skinny, clumsy boy from high school turned into such a beautiful man? He'd always been a nice, considerate person, though, and it appeared that those good characteristics remained.

"Sure. After all, you're helping me too."

They were already pulling up in front of the General Store.

"My pleasure," he assured her. "Come on. I have to drop you back at your car, too."

"And I really have to call home and tell Mom I'm running late. She probably expected me to be home by now."

It didn't take long for them to accomplish all their tasks. Kim asked Mrs. Young if she could use the phone, Greg and Mr. Young checked out the gardening supplies, and in no time at all Kim was the proud buyer of an electric hedge clipper for her mother.

"I know your Mom will like it, Kim," Mr. Young told her. "She's been eyeing it for the past few months, but didn't want to spend the money."

"I'm so glad Greg thought of it," Kim said.

She was still thanking him when they climbed back into the car for the trip back to the strip mall where they'd originally met. Kim was regretting leaving her car there, but she'd assumed they would be heading back to the shopping center to do their buying. She was sure Greg had thought the same thing. He finally convinced her to stop thanking him.

"After all, you're helping me too," he said. "This is a mutually advantageous arrangement."

"You're right." She shifted in the seat so she could look at Greg's profile while he drove. "Will you have time to get the thread tomorrow at lunch?"

"I'll just have to make time. There aren't many appointments scheduled, because I wanted to leave early. But you never know about emergencies."

Kim agreed. "Since we're out this way, I'll show you where the shop is so you'll be able to find it quickly. Keep going past the parking lot," she instructed.

Once she'd shown him the needlework shop, located in an old house just off the main street, they headed back toward the shopping center and her car.

"So, are you going to the Christmas pageant?" Greg asked, after a moment of silence.

"Are you kidding?" Kim asked. "My sister would kill me if I didn't go and see my niece and nephew sing in the angel chorus."

"So . . ." Greg's voice was hesitant. "Shall we go together?"

"You think we should?"

"Sure. Why not?" Greg shrugged. "My grandmother would like it, I'm sure. She mentioned your mom this morning, and they seem to be good friends. We could all go together."

Greg took his attention from the road for a brief moment, looking over at Kim with a grin.

"Everyone will be talking about us anyway, so we might as well give them something concrete to talk about." He smiled and her heart did a little flip.

"Okay." Kim felt herself smiling. "As you say, why not?"

"Great." He pulled into the shopping center lot just as they came to their agreement. The lot was still crowded with last-minute shoppers.

"We'll come by and pick you up, okay?" His smile was as warm as the noon sun.

"Okay. I'll tell Mom. She'll enjoy going with you guys," said Kim.

She wished him goodnight, then jumped out of the truck. As she let herself into her car, she looked back at Greg, politely waiting for her. He was such a gentleman. And he was newly settling in back in town. He was ready to find someone to spend his life with. Some woman in Malino was going to be so lucky.

As her engine turned over and she waved Greg off, Kim wondered if she could possibly be the one. She shook her head at her folly before pushing the gear into reverse.

As she checked traffic behind her before backing out, she wondered how she could even *think* that she might want another boyfriend. Not after the way she'd been treated by her last one!

Chapter Four

"So, how did your mother like the gift?"

It was early afternoon on Christmas Day, and Kim was surprised to hear Greg's voice on the phone. Her family had been expecting a call from her brother on the mainland, and his was the voice she'd expected to hear.

Yet, if she really thought about it, she should have known that Greg would call. She was just as curious to hear how his grandmother had liked the gift she'd chosen.

"She loved it. And your grandma?"

"She loved it." He laughed. "We did good."

She couldn't help joining his laughter. They were a good team, and she told him so.

"I think you're right," Greg agreed. "Vovo was overwhelmed. She loved the thread. She cried, Kim." His voice was totally serious now. Somber even. "And not because she was missing Mom."

Kim wasn't surprised at his grandmother's reaction. It wasn't the kind of present that usually occurred to a man.

"She kept going on about how surprised she was that I thought of it."

"And you took full credit, huh?"

Kim was glad to hear him laugh again.

"Hey, I tried. But she didn't believe for a moment that a guy like me would think of something like that, much less know where to go to buy it."

There was a short moment of silence on the line. Kim wished she could see him. Was he slouched in a chair? Or was he sitting at the kitchen table, all upright and proper? Or was he lying on his bed, as she was?

She pulled her mind away from that particular thought just as he offered his grandmother's *mahalo* for her help in choosing her present.

"Tell her it was my pleasure," she said. "Because it really was."

"I will. I think it made it even more special for her, the fact that it took two people to choose it."

Both of them considered this for a moment, enjoying that special Christmas pleasure of bringing happiness to others.

"So, what are you doing the rest of the day?" she asked.

It was a bright Hawaiian Christmas Day. The sun was shining, the palms trees swayed, the day was green and bright. *Mele Kalikimaka*, indeed, she thought.

But Greg didn't sound excited. "There's a family dinner coming up," he said dully.

Kim should have realized he would not be looking forward to that. It would be hard to forget the person missing from the dinner table. But she was gratified when she heard the cheer in his voice as he continued. She felt sure he was forcing it, but at least he was making an effort to enjoy the day.

"I guess you have one of those too," he said.

Kim deliberately kept her voice light. "Doesn't everyone?"

"We don't have any other family here, so it's just the three of us. Who all is coming to yours?"

"Just my sister and her family. My niece and nephew who sang last night," she reminded him. "And they'll bring my brother-in-law's uncle along. He's a widower and the only one of my brother-in-law's relatives on the Big Island. He's from Honolulu originally and most of his family is still there."

Kim scolded herself for babbling again, a habit she seemed to fall into regularly when speaking to Greg.

"That will be nice for you."

He knew Kim was smiling from the sound of her voice. He loved listening to her talk. As strange as it seemed, he could feel her happiness travel along the phone line, across the short distance from her house to his.

"It will be more than nice. Keith and Caitlin are at great ages for Christmas. We have all their gifts here so we can enjoy seeing them open them. It's such fun to watch children open gifts."

"Yeah. I wish we had some kids in the family."

Then, realizing that he was the only one available to provide those children, he quickly shifted the topic.

"I always wished I had brothers or sisters, too. But some things just don't work out."

"No," Kim agreed. "But it's not all fun and games having siblings, let me tell you. We got into our share of fights."

"Our neighbors invited us over for dinner," Greg said, changing the subject. "They thought it might be better for us to get out of the house—a change of scene, you know? But Vovo insisted on doing everything the way we always have."

There was a moment of silence. Kim let it run for a while. When she did speak, she kept her voice soft and as gentle as she could make it.

"I still remember that first Christmas after Dad died. Everything was so hard. He always took us to get the tree, then put it in the stand himself. That year Mom and I did it, but I could hardly see the screws on the darn tree stand because of the tears." Even now, after so many years, her voice caught as she remembered. "Almost everything we did for the holiday had the same kind of memories."

She heard his heavy sigh.

"It's the same here. We made an effort to keep things the same. Vovo said it was to honor her memory. But I wonder if she and Dad just don't have the courage to accept that she's really gone.

"They say there are these set stages you go through when you lose a loved one," he said. "I looked it up. There are five, and they can't say how long it takes to go through each one. It varies for everyone, I guess. But the final stage is acceptance."

"And you think celebrating the way your mother did is stopping you from accepting her death?"

"You don't think so?"

"No." Kim's voice was firm. "You *are* honoring her memory. I remember how much your mom liked Christmas. She especially loved making Christmas crafts and sharing her joy in them with everyone. I still remember how she taught me to make a beautiful wreath out of macadamia nut leaves one year. It was a special gift for my mother when I was a teenager and didn't have any money to buy a gift. My mom loved it, and your mom loved helping me with it. You did the right thing."

He didn't respond, and she wondered if he was ready to hang up. But finally his answer came.

"It doesn't make it any easier."

"No," Kim said. "It doesn't. And Christmas will always be bittersweet because she loved it so much. Next year it will be almost the same, though not quite as bad. Every year it will get a little easier, but you'll always miss her, especially at Christmastime."

Things were silent for a few seconds. In the other room, Kim's mother was playing Christmas carols on her old tape player. Kim had tried to switch her over to CDs, but Paula claimed to like her tape collection too much to give it up. Right now Kim could hear Bing Crosby crooning "White Christmas."

"My mother's playing 'White Christmas' in the other room," she said. "Why do you suppose 'White Christmas' is such a popular song in the islands? My mom just loves it. And she's never even seen snow."

Greg found himself smiling. His phone conversations with Kim had been a highlight of this past, very difficult, week. It wasn't only the way she could understand his loss because of her own, it was her quirky sense of looking at things.

"I've always liked it myself," he told her. "It's a nice song. And Mom loved it. That movie *White Christmas*? She loved it. Would make us all watch it several times every December."

"Did you watch it this year?" Kim asked.

He took his time with his response, and when it came his voice was low. "No."

"I don't blame you. I always cry when I see it, even though there aren't any particular memories associated with it for me. It's just such a touching story."

Another moment of silence stretched between them. Greg was comfortable with it, and thought Kim was okay with it too. At least she didn't rush to fill in the silence with useless words.

"So . . . when is your dinner?" she finally asked.

"Soon. Vovo's been cooking for a week, getting everything ready. She got up early this morning to make stuffing for the turkey. It smells really good in here right now, so I think it's about ready."

"It sounds good. Our house smells like turkey too."

"Uh oh, I'd better go. I see Vovo checking the oven. I think the turkey is done. I need to help her lift that heavy pan."

"Feel free to call again later," Kim said, "if you need to talk."

Greg was touched by her offer. "You'll be busy with your family."

"No problem. It's nice to have them around, but sometimes I need a little time away from them."

"I think I understand."

Boy, do I ever, Greg thought as he replaced the phone receiver. It was odd being back home after being away for so long. He'd been on his own for all those years during school. Sometimes he loved being back in Malino with his family around him. But at other times he thought he would explode if he didn't have some time to himself. Sometimes he just needed time alone—time to think, to brood, to grieve.

Greg was getting ready for bed when the phone rang. He managed to grab it on the second ring, worried that it might disturb his father and grandmother, who had retired early.

The perfect weather had not held, and rain fell on the corrugated roof, a sound he hoped had lulled them to peaceful sleep.

Somehow, he wasn't surprised to hear Kim's voice on the line.

"So how did it go?"

The fist that had held his heart tight since dinner loosened.

"It was okay."

Soft laughter came from the receiver, actually tickling his ear. He moved the receiver to his left ear, rubbing at his right. It was just a telephone. How could her laugh make his ear itch?

She was quiet for a while, but, as he'd noticed before, silences with Kim were far from uncomfortable. In fact, they were actually the opposite. He could imagine her at the other end of the line, her face serious as she thought about Christmases and lost parents.

"It's okay to cry, you know," she finally said. "Even macho guys do it sometimes."

Greg sighed. Kim had an uncanny way of knowing what he was thinking. Several times during the day he'd had to fight off tears. He'd been proud that he never did cry, but now he wondered if that was for the best.

"I know. My dad had tears in his eyes all day. But he doesn't let us see him actually cry. His generation didn't do that." He sighed. "Vovo was frenzied. She was so busy all day with cooking and activities that I don't think she had time to cry." He paused, releasing another heavy sigh. "I'm worried about what will happen now. The gifts are opened, the dinner is eaten. The wrappings are in the trash, the leftovers are in the refrigerator. The kitchen is spotless. She and Dad went in to bed a half hour ago, but I don't know if either of them is sleeping. I'm hoping Vovo will be so exhausted that she'll go right to sleep. And the rain might help."

"Yeah, it's always nice to go to sleep with the sound of rain on the roof. And you're aware of what she's doing," Kim assured him. "If she collapses, you'll hear her and can go in and give her a hug or something. If not, then she'll be fine."

"I'm sure you're right. She had some sleeping pills she

took for a while last summer. She might still have a few. She might have saved one for tonight."

Another of those silent moments elapsed while they listened to the falling rain. He couldn't help but compare the peace he felt in this conversation with the discomfort that had often filled him after a telephone conversation with Teri. It bothered him that he could now see how manipulative she'd been, because he hadn't seen it in the year they had dated. Another reason to avoid falling in love—it seemed love truly was blind. And how could a man make a proper choice when he couldn't see straight?

Pulling his mind from such troubling thoughts, Greg turned his attention back to his new friend.

"So, tell me how you've been managing."

"I'm fine. Christmas hasn't been a problem with us for the past couple of years. My dad's been gone for a while, and though we really miss him, it's not as fresh as your pain."

He could hear some faint noises from the other end and he pictured her rearranging herself on the chair. Or on the bed. Maybe moving the cat on or off her lap.

"The kids were such fun to have here. They got games that we played after dinner. And my brother called from the mainland to wish everyone a *Mele Kalikimaka*. We all had a lot of fun."

"Maybe a group game would have helped. We always give jigsaw puzzles for Christmas. It was a gift from Santa when I was young, and Mom always helped me with it. It got to be a family thing. But it's such a quiet pursuit."

"I got a jigsaw puzzle too, but I haven't even opened the box." Kim laughed. "And you're right about group games—it got pretty loud and wild."

"I don't think it would get wild at our house," Greg said. "I was thinking more like Monopoly or Scrabble."

She laughed again. "Having kids makes a big difference."

When she spoke again, Greg was surprised at the change in her tone.

"The really hard part comes next week."

"Next week?"

"New Year's Eve. Dad loved New Year's Eve. It's my birthday, you know."

"It is? No, I didn't know."

"Yep. New Year's Day. Dad loved firecrackers and cherry bombs and sky rockets and all that stuff. He just hated it when they started limiting what you could buy to use on your own. But he would always plan these big parties for my birthday. Once I got a little older, he would have it on New Year's Eve, with lots of fireworks. Didn't you come when we were in high school?"

"Now that you mention it, I think I did. How could I have forgotten it was a birthday party?"

"Easy. It was a long time ago."

"So, do you still have a big party?"

"No. Mom and I don't want to fool with fireworks, and there isn't much you can get these days anyway. And then with the big town party this year, it's a whole different thing. I was thinking of inviting a few people over on Wednesday for an open house. I thought I could cook up some stuff, make a big cake . . ."

"You shouldn't have to do all that for your own birthday."

Kim laughed. "Mom will help. But I like to cook. It's my hobby. I like reading cookbooks and finding new recipes, and trying out different things with old ones. I can even decorate a cake and have it turn out looking darn good, if I do say so myself."

"I believe you." Greg laughed. Then he realized what

he'd just done: he'd laughed. On Christmas, a miserable day if ever there was one, now that his mother was no longer there to share it with her family. And though they'd tried to celebrate in her honor, the strain had shown. But now he was laughing. Suddenly, it was like any other day.

"You are a multi-talented woman, Kim Ascension."

For a moment he wondered if his tone was too somber, that it would cramp the lightness of the conversation. But Kim came through for him again.

"Darn right," she replied.

This time they laughed together. Afterward, they shared a quiet moment.

When Greg broke the silence, his voice was barely audible. "Thank you, Kim."

She didn't pretend to not know what he was talking about. She spoke immediately.

"No thanks necessary. I'm glad you're feeling better. Try to keep that in mind as you close your eyes tonight. Up in heaven, your mom is smiling too. She was there with you all day today, and she loved every minute." Her voice dropped for a moment, then became firm in its conviction. "And now she's smiling, too, because she can hear your wonderful laughter."

Greg was so touched he couldn't speak. As if she realized that it was time for him to be alone with his thoughts, Kim said a soft goodbye and hung up.

Greg put the receiver back into its cradle, then walked out into the hall that connected the bedrooms. He paused outside his grandmother's door, almost holding his breath as he listened. All seemed quiet. A good sign, he was sure.

He continued on to his father's room, where he repeated his action. When the result was the same, he returned to his room and undressed. As he pulled the covers up a few minutes later, Greg's last thoughts were of Kim Ascension.

How had he not remembered what a special person she was?

"Working hard?" Greg asked, appearing out of nowhere.

Kim she glanced around the bank. Not a soul stood in the lobby. She was alone behind the teller's counter, while Sandy and Nishiko were busy at their desks.

"Not especially. As you can see," she added, raising a hand to gesture at the quiet room, "I think everyone is in Hilo or Kona shopping at the after-Christmas sales."

Greg smiled. "Or returning the things they got."

Kim took his deposit, smiling as she checked his numbers. "Not *our* giftees."

"Giftees?"

Kim looked up just in time to catch his incredible grin. Had Greg had this wonderful grin in high school? How could she not have noticed? It made his eyes twinkle in the most tantalizing manner, and the merest suggestion of a dimple cracked his cheek. He was clean-shaven today, but a hint of stubble showed in the afternoon.

She had to pull herself out of her reverie in order to answer him.

"Sure, why not? If it's not a word, it should be one."

Kim watched his smile widen.

"Well, whatever you call them, I know my grandmother, the giftee, is very happy. She's still telling me what a special gift that was. I'm sure you'll hear all about it the next time she comes in here."

His expression became serious as his voice grew softer. "I hadn't realized until I saw her sewing these past few days . . . but she hadn't been. Sewing, I mean. Not since I moved back in last summer. So I have to thank you doubly."

"You're very welcome," Kim said.

"I mean it." A wrinkle appeared at the center of his forehead as his eyebrows drew together. "Not only for steering me toward the perfect gift, but for getting her back into a hobby she enjoyed. It means a lot to me to see her acting like her old self."

Kim shook her head at him. "You don't have to keep thanking me. I was happy to help. And remember, you did the same for me."

"I don't know. Somehow I think my situation was much more severe. I think you've pushed Vovo into the next stage of grief."

Kim stared at him for a moment, then reached into her drawer and removed some bills.

Greg watched her as she began to count the money. Her head was tilted so that he could see only the top of her head. A rich, dark brown, her hair was thick with a slight wave to it. It shone darkly in the bank's light, deep auburn highlights winking out. It just reached her shoulders, and he couldn't help wondering what it would look like longer, reaching down the length of her back.

"Here you are."

Kim's words brought Greg's mind back to the present as she handed him his deposit receipt and some cash. He watched her hands again as she counted out the bills a second time.

"Thank you." He had to smile. He'd smiled more in the last few days than he had in the past four months. Kim was really good for him. "It seems all I do these days is thank you for something or other."

Kim grinned at him, an impish look in her eye. "Nothing wrong with that. I don't mind having a man in my debt."

Greg folded the receipt and bills into his wallet, but didn't move away from the counter. "I guess you've heard about the town party on New Year's Eve?"

Kim's eyes sparkled.

Greg shook his head. "You mentioned it on the phone the other day, didn't you?"

She looked like she wanted to laugh, but she didn't. She just nodded and continued to smile. "Everyone who comes in talks about it. It was a good idea, and sounds like it will be a lot of fun."

"Want to go?"

Kim blinked up at him. "With you?"

He grinned at her. "With me."

"Like a date?"

His grin faded a little. Didn't she want to go with him? All his eighteen-year-old insecurities about women flooded back.

"I guess so. I'll pick you up at your house and we can walk over. What do you think?"

"Okay."

Her smile faded a bit as well. "Since this is a brand new activity for the town, there won't be any childhood memories to turn me nostalgic and teary. Also, Dad wouldn't have liked it as much as doing the fireworks himself. So I think I'll be able to enjoy it very much."

There was still no one waiting behind him, so Greg didn't feel the need to hurry off. He leaned an elbow on the counter.

"Okay. I'll be at your house on Tuesday evening then. Think your mother will want to come?"

Kim shook her head. "No. She usually spends New Year's Eve quietly at home. But I will ask her. It's nice of you to think of her."

The smile he received made Greg glow inside.

"I'll pack a picnic dinner," Kim continued. "That's what most of the people are doing, you know. And we'll probably not want to walk over. We'll need quilts or blankets or chairs to sit on, and food and drinks. There will be a lot to lug over."

"Good point. Okay, I'll bring the truck."

Kim gave him a considering look before she spoke again. "People will talk, you know."

"I know."

"Will it be all right?"

"Of course. I'm a big boy. Besides, they're already talking. I've had several comments since the Christmas pageant."

"You have?"

"Oh, yeah. Mrs. Yoshida was the latest. She brought in her cat for his shots this morning and told me how disappointed she was that I'd found a girl before she had a chance to introduce me to her granddaughter."

"You're kidding!"

She looked startled, and an equally startling thought occurred to Greg. "*You* don't mind, do you?"

Here he was feeling magnanimous because he didn't care what people thought if they went on a "date" to watch the fireworks display. But it could well be a problem for Kim. He already knew she didn't have a boyfriend at the moment, but that didn't mean that she wanted to associate with him all the time in public, where everyone could see them together. The wedding in Hilo was different, since the people who would see them there were not local.

"No, no, of course not." Kim seemed embarrassed that he would ask.

Greg breathed a sigh of relief, but he wanted this new wrinkle ironed out.

"Ah, will it be a problem for you—being paired up with me, I mean?"

Kim stared blankly at him.

Greg almost stammered in his embarrassment, but he felt

he owed it to Kim to mention this, now that he'd thought of it. "I mean, if you and I are paired off by everyone in town, you won't have a chance to meet anyone new."

Kim surprised him by laughing. "There isn't 'anyone new,' Greg, and not likely to be. Besides, you might understand when I tell you that I'm a bit disillusioned with men right now."

He nodded. But it gave him a special feeling to know she still wanted to see him, even if she wasn't impressed with the male gender as a whole.

Greg glanced at his watch. "It's almost six. You'll be getting off soon, right?"

"Yep. Why?" Kim glanced at her watch as well, as though surprised at the late hour.

"Well, it's Friday night. That means leftovers at my house. I wondered if you'd be interested in having dinner with me? I've got a real craving for pizza. We could drive over to the Paniolo Inn."

"Oh, my gosh, that sounds so good," Kim said. "But I'm shocked at you, Greg Yamamoto. Don't you want to take your grandmother?"

It took a second for Greg to realize that she was kidding with him, but as soon as he did he found himself laughing again.

"I do love her, but I see her across the table from me at almost every meal. Tonight I was hoping for youth and beauty."

"Youth and beauty, huh?" She grinned at him, blinking in a highly exaggerated fashion. "I must say, you have a way with words, Dr. Yamamoto."

"So, is that a yes?"

The grin faded, and Kim the professional banker was back. "It is. But you realize that I can't leave as soon as the doors close. I have to cash out the drawer and close up and everything."

"No problem. I'll just stroll over to the General Store and pick up a few things I need."

Kim bestowed a brilliant smile on him as he turned away. If it had already been dark outside, it would have been enough to light his route all the way to the store.

The drive to Kamuela was pleasant. In fact, Kim was beginning to think that everything about Greg was pleasant. Could he be for real? So far, it seemed that he was.

They drove out in his truck, enjoying conversation on the way. Mostly, they caught up on the years they'd missed. Greg talked about Honolulu and animals he'd cared for. The discussion continued over dinner, expanding to include movies and music.

Finally, Kim pushed her plate away. "That was the best pizza I've ever had." Her hand dropped down to her stomach, which she felt sure would measure at least an inch larger than it had an hour ago.

"I agree," Greg said. "I can't remember when I've enjoyed a meal so much."

Kim waved her hand at him. "Oh, that. Me too. That's the company." She grinned.

He grinned back. "I'm sure you're right."

Their waitress appeared and began to clear away their plates. "Would you like any dessert?" she asked.

"Kim?" Greg asked.

"You must be kidding. I haven't any room for dessert. I probably won't have room for breakfast, I ate so much."

The waitress left their table laughing. Greg, too, was smiling.

"I like to see a woman who enjoys her food."

"Dated some anorexic types in Honolulu, did you?"

"One or two."

"Boy, we sure do know how to pick them, don't we?" Kim leaned back in her chair, relaxing after the delicious meal. "I get an impulsive romantic who falls in love with a woman he's never seen before. You get thin women who don't eat."

"But we're doing okay at present," Greg said. "So let's just forget about those others. What do you say?"

"Sounds good to me."

Kim actually felt drunk even though she hadn't had even a beer. She'd stuck to iced tea, yet she still felt like she was flying. *It must be happiness,* she decided.

But as Greg paid for their meal, her mood plummeted as quickly as it had soared. What was she doing, flying wild with happiness? She was just out with an old friend, that's all. Neither of them wanted to get serious. They both had had too many problems in their recent personal lives to even *try* getting involved.

So what the heck was she doing?

Chapter Five

"Ready to go?"

It was almost dark on New Year's Eve. Greg stood at Kim's door—the side door that opened into the kitchen, not the "formal" door at the front of the house. No one used that door except the odd stranger in town, usually some nice clean-cut young men out proselytizing.

"Just about." Kim moved aside so that Greg could enter the kitchen. "Come on in. I'll need you to help with the stuff."

"The stuff?"

"You know, the food, blankets, folding chairs. Stuff."

Paula was in the kitchen with Kim, washing dishes at the sink. She called out a hello, and he responded in kind.

"Want to come with us, Mrs. Ascension? Plenty of room on the blanket. I'll even let you have my chair."

"No." Paula had a girlish giggle of a laugh. "You silly boy. You young people go on and have lots of fun."

Kim bundled the last of the things into the cooler on the counter. "Did you ask your father and grandmother if they wanted to come?"

"I did," he said, "and their answers were surprisingly similar to your mother's." He grinned at Paula and she grinned back.

"We too old to go out all night like you and Kim."

Greg felt it necessary to protest. "You aren't old, Mrs. Ascension. You're a very attractive mature woman who is young at heart."

Once again he was rewarded with her youthful laugh.

"See what I mean?" Greg told her. "If I heard that laugh of yours from the other room, I'd think there was a teenager in here with Kim."

"See, Ma, haven't I been telling you?"

Kim turned to Greg. "Hiram Ah Yo has been after her to go out with him. And she keeps saying she's too old to date."

"Shame on you, Mrs. A. Shattering the poor man's dreams."

Greg's voice held a teasing tone that made Kim's mother blush. She looked a lot like her daughter when she was laughing in that carefree way.

"He's a nice man too," Kim said.

Greg nodded. "I know him. He brings his cat to the clinic."

"He has a cat?" Paula asked. Her eyes sparkled with interest.

"See? You've been turning him down and you don't know anything about him."

Kim turned to Greg. "He does the landscaping at the medical center, so she sees him at work all the time."

Greg nodded. "He does the work at the clinic too. He's a good man. His cat is a huge male, spayed, of course, with the most beautiful markings. He's a gray tiger, short-haired."

Paula didn't say a word, but she was listening closely. Kim bit back a smile. Her mother cherished the two cats they owned. Perhaps this insight into Hiram's character would sway her toward accepting the next time he asked her to join him for dinner at the seafood place. Her grin grew wider when Paula asked Greg a question.

"Is his cat prettier than our Sammy?"

Hearing his name, the gray tiger under the table stretched out and then sauntered over to Paula, winding himself around her ankles.

"Sammy is a beauty, no doubt of that, with gorgeous markings. But he's much smaller, and his coloring is completely different from Hiram's cat. Did you know his cat is also named Sammy? It's a popular name for cats."

Paula was obviously surprised. Kim almost laughed at the look on her mother's face. The similarity in their cats, the serendipity of their names . . .

Kim was sure her mother would speak of it to Hiram. She wished she could be there.

Kim knew Hiram from the bank, as he had been a customer there for many years. In fact, she'd never mentioned it to her mother, but Hiram had quietly asked her permission last year before he ever asked Paula for a date. Kim had been very impressed with his quiet yet distinguished manner.

Thinking about her mother on a date made her mouth curve into a secretive little smile. When Kim caught Greg watching her, she winked at him, then reached for her sweater and jacket, both draped over the back of a kitchen chair. The weather had been beautiful so far; the sun had shone all day and there had been nary a cloud in sight. But it would get cold as the evening drew on.

Most of the townspeople would be heading out to the

park about now. There would be live music all evening, followed by the fireworks display at midnight to welcome in the new year.

Greg and Kim had decided to follow the general plan. There was sure to be dancing and lots of friendly visiting.

"Well, I'm ready. Shall we go?" Kim said.

Greg reached for the cooler on the counter before she could ask him to take it. Kim smiled her thanks, hugged her mother, then followed Greg outside.

She laughed. "You really meant it when you said you'd bring the truck."

"Yeah. I guess I could have borrowed Dad's sedan, but I didn't think of it." He shrugged. It was too late now. "Do you have a problem with the truck? It can be hard for smaller people to get in and out, but you've ridden in it before. And I'd be happy to give you a boost if you need it."

"Hey! I'm not going to let a little thing like my height dictate what I'll ride in."

Greg laughed. "Atta girl."

Despite Kim's determination, it was a long step from the ground to the seat, and her legs weren't nearly as long as she wished. Greg could feel the warmth of her body as he supported her, one hand on her arm, the other against her back.

When she started to slip, his hand slid over to her hip, giving him a firmer hold. Although she was thin, his hand rested on the warm, firm softness of her hip. No bones, thank goodness. Another point in her favor. He liked a nicely rounded figure, and hated the bony look that fashion models and actresses promoted and Teri had dieted to maintain.

There was a lot he liked about Kim, he realized. She dressed comfortably and always looked good. This evening she wore jeans and sneakers, with a long-sleeved cotton knit top. He'd made note of the extra coverings she brought along, though he thought he would have enjoyed keeping her warm later.

Once he had climbed into the truck for the short drive to the park, Kim was anxious to discuss her mother and Hiram.

"I'm so glad you mentioned Hiram has a cat. He seems like such a nice man, and I've told Ma she should go out when he asks. But so far she's said no. Maybe this will push her to say yes."

She looked out the window for a while, watching a group of teenagers walking toward the park.

"I don't mind if she doesn't want to get married again, but I think she could certainly have some fun with a man once in a while. It's been a long time since Dad died. They used to like to go to the movies, but she hardly ever goes any more. I've invited her to come with me, but she says she doesn't want to interfere when I go with my friends."

"I'm sure my father will be the same way eventually. It's hard to start dating again after being married to the same person for so long. My grandmother never dated or anything after my grandfather died."

"But she was older, wasn't she, when he died? My mother was only fifty-one when dad died. She's only fifty-six now."

Their arrival at the park stopped the discussion of their parents and grandparents. Many people were already there. Blankets were spread in prime spots, and chairs and coolers were in abundant supply. Some families were already eating.

Greg and Kim took their things from the truck, looking around for an empty place to sit. As they stood at the edge of the parking lot, Kim saw her friend Emma waving frantically. She and her family were already established in a lovely area beneath a false kamani tree with a great view of the raft anchored out on the ocean where the fireworks would be discharged.

"Over there," she said, gesturing to Greg with her head. "See where Emma and Matt are? She must have saved us a spot."

Emma was there with Matt, her mother, and her son, Devin. Her mother would take the baby home later so they could stay for the midnight show.

"I'm too old and he's too young to stay up to usher in the new year," Mrs. Lindsey said.

"You sound like my mother," Kim told her with a laugh.

"Mine would have said the same," Greg said.

He and Kim exchanged a brief look. Things were looking up for him, if he could speak about her so calmly, and without feeling as though his heart would break. With Kim's help and practical outlook, Greg thought that he might actually be at the final stage of grief—acceptance. If not, he was darned close.

"Look at that dog," Emma said, bringing everyone's attention to a German shepherd playing in the breaking waves. "We would have liked to bring Poki, but all the ads said not to. Poor thing, he hated being left behind."

"But you did the right thing," Greg said. "Dogs can get very upset when fireworks go off. They can run away and get lost. It's much better to leave them at home in their familiar environment. I hope the owner of that beautiful animal plans to take him home before midnight."

He then busied himself with the blanket and didn't notice the approving look that Emma threw Kim's way.

The evening passed quickly and pleasantly. They shared all their food, listened to the bands and vocalists, and marveled at how cooperative the weather was being.

Before long Sonia was wrapping a sleepy Devin in his blanket and taking him home to bed.

"I'll keep him at my place tonight, so you two don't have to worry about him, okay?" she said.

While Emma and Matt walked Sonia to her car, Kim and Greg remained on their blanket, listening to the music. A local man played slack key guitar.

"He's good," Greg commented. "I had no idea he even played."

Kim nodded. "I've heard him before."

Greg offered her another soda, and she accepted.

"So, tell me about your party," he said. "Have you been cooking all day?"

Kim smiled. "Couldn't. I had to work. Otherwise, I would have. I did make some potato salad, and I have a ham in the oven. Ma said she'd take it out for me when the timer went off."

Greg enjoyed watching her face as she talked about the food. There was no denying the joy that shone from her face as she told him about the menu she'd planned for the next day.

"Over the weekend, I made some quick breads—banana and zucchini and one with pineapple and coconut. The cake is in the freezer and I'll ice it and decorate it in the morning. It's easier to decorate when it's frozen," she told him. "It's a marble cake."

Greg had to grin. "Can't make up your mind whether you like vanilla or chocolate better?"

"Oh, you." Kim hit him over the head with her folded napkin.

"Looks like we got back just in time." Matt Correa's voice caught them off guard.

"Just a friendly exchange of words," Greg said.

* * *

The time passed quickly, and soon the fireworks began. It started slowly, a few minutes before midnight. A few small displays, built to a crescendo at the stroke of midnight, and continued on for another fifteen minutes. Kim rested comfortably alongside Greg. He had pulled her against his shoulder right after the display began. She made a half-hearted attempt to pull away, then gave up. Why bother? It was dark, no one was paying attention, and she was much warmer, not to mention more comfortable.

It took Kim a moment to realize that Emma and Matt had disappeared. Could they have left for home without saying goodbye? She looked around, noting that their blanket and cooler were still nearby.

Surprised, Kim looked around and caught sight of Emma walking toward her. Matt was behind her with Mele and Ben. Mele was holding something.

Greg pulled her to her feet just as the others arrived at the blanket. They had attracted a crowd as they walked over, and there were a lot of people watching when Emma finally approached Kim.

Suddenly, there came a loud "Surprise!" from a dozen voices. Then they broke into a rousing chorus of "Happy Birthday."

Kim stood statue-still, motionless with shock. Mele walked forward with her burden, a large sheet cake with "Happy New Year and Happy Birthday Kim" written across the top.

Tears stung her eyes. All around her, Kim could see the familiar faces of the town residents—neighbors, bank customers, old school friends and childhood playmates. And her mother!

"Ma?"

Her mother grinned happily at her. "I had a nap. I couldn't miss my daughter's surprise party, now could I?"

"Oh, my . . ."

Nothing more would come. Kim wasn't sure she'd ever been rendered speechless before, but at the moment she was too stunned to come up with words.

"I guess we managed to surprise you," Emma said.

The group around them laughed.

"You did." Kim tried to laugh, but tears threatened instead. She was touched and her emotions were fragile. "Thank you."

"It was Greg's idea," Mele said.

Kim turned toward Greg, blinking rapidly in hopes of stemming the tears. "Thank you," she repeated, softer this time.

Then she gestured to the cake. "Let's eat. I take it someone thought to bring a knife and some plates?"

The items were produced, but not handed over until candles were lit and Kim had blown them out. Once again tears stung her eyes as she cut into the large cake. "This is so nice of you all."

As soon as Kim put the first piece of cake on a plate, Mele took the knife from her and thrust the newly filled plate into her hands instead. "Now you go sit down and enjoy this, and let everyone wish you a happy birthday. Go on."

With a real laugh this time—the tears happily gone—Kim took her cake and returned to her blanket. For another hour, she sat with her friends and neighbors, reminiscing about the recent Christmas holiday and the gifts they'd received.

It was almost two when Greg dropped Kim back at her house.

"I don't know how you're going to manage that open house tomorrow," he said, his expression showing his concern. "I suppose you plan to cook a whole bunch more, but you need to get some sleep."

Kim smiled. She felt so dreamily happy. "I doubt I could get to sleep right now anyway. I won't stay up too long. I think I'll bake some cookies; I find it relaxing."

"If you say so." Greg brought the cooler in from the truck and helped her unpack it. Then he left, telling her he'd see her the next day.

"At least you told people to come after one," he said.

Kim laughed. "Hey, it's New Year's Day. I knew everyone would be up late."

Greg stood just inside the door for a moment, looking uncertain. Finally, he took hold of Kim's shoulders and pulled her slightly forward. She watched as his head lowered, mesmerized by his eyes as they grew larger and larger as he drew closer. His eyes were so dark she couldn't tell the iris from the pupil. But she could see her reflection there, growing larger and larger.

Finally, their faces were so close, Kim just closed her eyes. His lips met her skin, butterfly light and cool to the touch. His kiss was gentle and tender—and on her forehead.

Her eyes fluttered open.

"Happy New Year, Kim," Greg said.

He looked into her eyes, then lowered his head again. Kim couldn't believe how much she wanted his next kiss to be on her lips.

"Happy Birthday."

His voice was as soft as a mountain breeze, as warm as the gentle tradewinds. He brought his lips to hers. They were soft and warm and slightly sweet—no doubt from the cake they'd eaten a short while ago. Kim's lips felt tingly with the possibilities.

But Greg didn't seem to feel them. He pulled away, wished her a happy birthday again, and was gone.

Kim stood at the door for a full minute, savoring the moment. She'd never forget this night. The fireworks, the surprise party, and now Greg's brief kiss. She was so happy she felt ready to burst. How could she possibly go to sleep now?

Turning into the kitchen, Kim rifled through her recipe file until she found one for sugar cookies. Rolling out dough and choosing designs from her collection of cookie cutters was a sure route to peaceful relaxation.

Humming happily, she began to pull out the ingredients. She couldn't remember when she'd had such a nice start to her birthday. The year ahead was sure to be a good one since it had started out so splendidly.

"So, what do you think about Greg?" Emma asked. "Planning the surprise party and all?"

The two women were alone in the Ascensions' kitchen on New Year's Day. Kim's birthday open house was in full swing and, although her friends tried to keep her in the midst of the party and out of the kitchen, she continued to escape there. Her friends just didn't seem to understand that puttering in the kitchen wasn't "work" for her. She loved it.

Kim's face lit up at Emma's question, and her friend laughed. "I can see the answer in your face. So you like him, hmm?"

Kim's smile faded. "Of course I like him. What's not to like?"

She opened a bag of melon balls she'd taken from the refrigerator and poured them into a glass bowl.

"It's just that I'm not ready for a relationship, and I don't think he is either. Right now what we both need is friendship. And so far, that's what we've been for each other—friends."

Emma's grin widened. "I'm a big believer in friendship with the male gender," she said.

Her statement was punctuated by a loud pop as she opened a bag of chips.

Kim laughed. Matt and Emma had been the best of friends for years before their marriage.

"In fact, who knows where this friendship will lead?" Emma continued, upending the newly opened bag over a large plastic bowl. The chips tumbled out, filling the bowl to the brim. Emma took one and bit into it.

"Just leave yourself open, Kim," she advised. "Eventually, you and Greg might find yourselves more than just friends."

"I don't want to worry about going beyond that," Kim insisted. "We've been good for one another. I really like talking to him, and he seems to feel the same way. I'm perfectly happy with that."

Emma didn't have a chance say more. Paula came into the kitchen with Violet and scolded Kim.

"Shame on you, Kim, hiding in here. You should be out there enjoying your party." Paula put the bowl of fruit salad into her daughter's hands and gave her a gentle push toward the door.

"Go, go. You take her, Emma," she said. "Leave the kitchen to us old ladies."

Laughing, they all pushed Kim out the door.

"It's my turn to ask a favor."

Greg had run into Kim at the park and talked her into

walking over to the Dairy Queen for a milkshake. Greg had been jogging, Kim taking a power walk. It was the first Saturday of the new year—a beautiful, sunny day.

"A favor?" Kim repeated. "Sure. Anything."

Greg grinned. "Anything?"

His suggestive leer just made her laugh. She knew better than to be taken in by it. He was too much of a sweetheart to take advantage of her. Look at that great surprise he'd planned for her on New Year's Eve. He'd come by the next day with a gift of new, nonstick cookie sheets for her birthday. It still gave her a thrill just to remember it, such a special, perfect gift.

"You shouldn't be so quick to agree," Greg insisted.

The New Year's kiss suddenly came to mind, and Kim felt her cheeks turn hot. It had been such an innocent kiss, but she'd felt herself longing for more, despite her sincere words to Emma about keeping her relationship with Greg to pure friendship. So she kept her head down, pulling the plastic straw in and out of the thick drink.

"You can't fool me," she said. "Besides, I owe you for agreeing to be my date for the wedding. And I'm not even mentioning the wonderful gift you brought for my birthday even though I said *no gifts*." Her head came back up.

Greg didn't look the least bit miffed by her scolding.

"Hey, I saw other people bringing you gifts. And I know it's something you'll use. I saw those heaps of cookies you baked."

Kim's cheeks felt warm as she recalled how late—or how *early*—she'd been up on New Year's Day, baking tray after tray of cookies.

"I love the pans. It's just that you shouldn't have." She dipped her straw again, unable to swirl it through the thick shake. "My sister just gave me a CD."

"I wanted to."

His sincere answer created a warm glow that settled over her like an old shawl.

"Thank you again."

Then she smiled at him, a mischievous grin that brought an instant response to his lips.

"Most of the other guests brought food of some kind. I just put it all out to share, but I still have leftovers, if you want to come by for dinner. Lots of leftovers."

"I just might," he told her, grinning back. "So don't issue an invitation lightly."

Kim sobered, but she continued to meet his eyes.

"No problem."

Sitting across from one another at the small table, they ignored their drinks while continuing to stare into each other's eyes.

There was no telling how long they might have remained that way if a young boy with his arms full of hamburgers and fries hadn't bumped into their table, jostling their drinks.

"Sorry," he mumbled, and hurried off, red with embarrassment.

Greg watched him for a moment before turning back to Kim.

"Man, I remember those days. See how tall and skinny he is? I'll bet he's clumsy all the time, because he still hasn't gotten used to having such long legs. I hope he gets over it quicker than I did."

"I don't recall you being clumsy."

Greg's eyes widened in disbelief. "Oh, come on now. I know what a klutz I was when I was young. I grew so much the year I was sixteen, I just couldn't seem to control my arms and legs. The coach tried to talk me into trying out for basketball, but I knew I'd just make a fool of myself. And I did," he added with a wry smile.

"But aren't all boys a bit awkward at that age?"

"That's putting it gently." Greg smiled at her, a sweet, tender smile, not remotely like the cynical one he'd offered a minute earlier. "I was never very coordinated, and I don't know why everyone thought I would suddenly be a jock when I'd never shown any aptitude for sports in my previous sixteen years."

Now it was Greg's turn to concentrate on his paper cup.

"Dad was so proud that the coach approached me. He and I shot baskets over at the school for a week beforehand. And of course, I was awful. But I made the team anyway. I don't know why."

Kim thought she did. "I'll bet the coach saw something there that he felt he could work on. Look at you now." She ran her gaze over the part of his body visible above the table. "You could pass for a jock now, no problem. He might have seen that in you, and hoped it would come out."

Greg frowned. "Maybe. But it sure didn't appear in high school. I sat on the bench for most of the games. I would have quit, but Dad was so proud. He used to go to all the games."

Kim nodded, but she thought she could see something else in his troubled expression.

"Wasn't he proud when you won the science fair?"

A quick grin transformed Greg's face. "You remember that?"

"Sure. You were my prize pupil, if you recall. I was proud of all your accomplishments."

She watched him put the straw to his lips, pulling at the thick liquid. He hadn't answered, or had he?

"So . . . was your dad proud of your academic achievements?"

"Stubborn, aren't you?"

Kim just grinned.

"Okay. To answer your question, yes and no. He and Mom were both proud of anything I did. But there was something there that I knew but can't really explain. I just knew Dad liked the fact that I was on the basketball team more than he liked the way I always won the science fair."

"It's that old guy thing," Kim said. "It's something he could brag about to all his buddies. Some of them might not think much of a brainy kid who wins scholastic awards, but all guys seem to admire an athlete."

Greg nodded.

Kim examined him closely. That was probably as much introspection as he cared to indulge in for one day.

"So what did you want to talk to me about?"

Greg gave her a quizzical look. "Sorry?"

Kim had to laugh. "When we ran into each other earlier. Remember? Something about a favor?"

Now it was Greg's turn to laugh.

"You're right. You got me so distracted, I almost forgot." His lips quirked as he looked into her eyes. "You have the strangest effect on me, Kim Ascension. You get me to thinking, for one thing. And you make me feel happy, for another."

"Why, thank you. That's the nicest thing anyone's ever said to me."

They smiled at one another, the noise of the busy Dairy Queen retreating into the distance. Finally, Greg returned to their original subject.

"As for that favor you so rashly promised . . ."

Kim laughed.

"I started thinking on Thursday night."

"Uh oh."

He smiled at her words but continued. "You did such a

great job with your open house," he said, shaking his head. "I still can't believe you did all that work for your own birthday party."

Kim shrugged. He was so full of compliments today; she was beginning to feel embarrassed. "I like to cook. Much more than my mom even."

"Anyway, the success of your party gave me an idea." Greg waited until she looked back up at him before continuing.

"Vovo's birthday is on January twelfth. Her seventy-fifth. Would you help me plan a party for her? Do the food and all? I'll pay you for the supplies and everything."

"Don't be silly." Kim's first response was to refuse payment. Her second was quite different. "You're so sweet to think of something like this. She'll be so thrilled."

Greg didn't look too happy at her assessment of him. "I hope she'll be happy. She needs that right now. And," Greg's tone was adamant, "I insist on paying you for supplies. If you do it," he added. "I couldn't let you use your own money for a party I'm more or less asking you to cater."

"Of course I'll do it." Kim grinned. "I'll even let you pay for 'supplies,' since you put it that way." She laughed. "It almost sounds like a new career."

Greg couldn't help a grin of his own. "Somehow, I don't think there would be a whole lot of business for a caterer here in Malino."

"You're right. What was I thinking?" She rolled her eyes. "So, a birthday party for your grandmother. What did you want me to do?"

"The twelfth is on a Sunday this year, so it's a perfect day for a party. And seventy-five seems like a milestone of some kind." Greg said. "I was thinking that I could get Dad to lure her out of the house, and we could set up. The same kind of thing you did for your party. I'll invite all her friends."

"I know you didn't think much of me calling you sweet, but that's what you are. This is such a nice thing you're going to do for your grandmother." She almost got tears in her eyes thinking about it.

Greg looked embarrassed by her praise. He ducked his head toward his drink.

"I'm hoping it will distract her from thinking about how she's still alive and her daughter isn't." His voice was grim.

"Umm." Kim hid her smile. She knew he was a warm-hearted guy trying hard not to show it. Why did men think it was weak to show their emotions? Personally, Kim thought it made a man stronger to admit that he could feel as well as perform feats of strength.

She stirred her shake with the straw while she thought about the party. "I can get my mom to help. She and your grandmother are friends, maybe she can ask her over or something. You know, if you have the party on Saturday, it might be even better. I can get Ma to take her to the needlework shop. She can ask her to help her choose some yarn or something. Then we can set up while they're gone."

"That sounds great. It should be a real surprise, too, since it will be a day early."

Their eyes met and she could see relief and gratitude there. There was always so much gratitude flowing between them. Unfortunately, she wanted more than gratitude.

Startled at her inner thoughts, Kim remembered Emma's laughing warnings about male friends. She liked having Greg for a friend, but even a friendship shouldn't be based solely on gratitude. She wasn't after a *romantic* relationship. But they had to move beyond gratitude.

Unfortunately, that would have to wait.

"So . . ." she said. "What do you think she'd like to eat at her party?"

Chapter Six

Vovo's party went off without a hitch. Paula invited her old friend to help her choose fibers for a needlework canvas, and Violet was glad to oblige.

It was another success for Kim, who was gaining an impressive reputation as both a cook and a party planner. But she was beginning to worry about Greg's penchant for thanking her several times in every conversation they shared. Even for a couple who were just friends, it was a bit much. She'd become attached enough to Greg that she hoped their friendship would survive beyond Crystal's wedding. So far, it looked good, but Kim was afraid that if his feelings for her were all about gratitude, eventually he'd feel too guilty to even look at her.

Kim didn't know how to solve this, and it troubled her. And once again it was a holiday—this time, the three-day Martin Luther King, Jr. weekend. It would have been nice to have three days solely for relaxing, but Kim didn't think she'd have much time for that. She'd be driving back and forth to Hilo all weekend—or at least it would feel that way. Scheduled bridesmaid duties filled her weekend.

Greg had been shocked when she told him about her weekend plans during a phone conversation on Wednesday night. He'd called to thank her yet again for the success of his grandmother's party. Kim had gritted her teeth and tried not to scream. She really had to find another way for him to help her so that she could turn the tables and thank him.

But for now, she just had to endure his gratitude.

"She enjoyed the party so much, she cries every time she talks about it," he had said. "I think that's good." He sounded uncertain.

"It's wonderful," Kim assured him, working hard to relax her jaw muscles. Talking to Greg used to be relaxing, but all this gratitude was becoming stressful.

"So what are you doing this weekend?" Greg had asked.

Kim wondered if he was thinking of asking her to do something with him. She would have loved it; unfortunately, she wouldn't have the time.

"I'll be busy pretty much all weekend with bridesmaid duties."

"Bridesmaid duties?" he repeated. "What on earth are those?"

Kim smiled. Guys didn't know anything about weddings and the rituals that went with them.

"Well, when you become a bridesmaid you have to do certain things for the bride. Like help her get dressed and stuff."

"Okay. That makes sense, I guess. But it's a bit early for that, isn't it?"

"The maid of honor has the most things to do, and one of those is to plan the bridal shower and bachelorette party."

There was no reaction from Greg on that bit of information.

"We're going in to pick up our dresses on Monday," Kim

continued. "Crystal is actually flying the out-of-town girls in for this. That's why she picked the holiday weekend for our final visit with the seamstress."

Kim heard a whistle from Greg. She didn't blame him. Crystal's lifestyle was unlike anyone else's in her small island sphere.

"Is this Crystal independently wealthy?"

"Crystal isn't, at least not yet. But her parents are. They both come from very wealthy families on the East Coast. Or at least, Crystal said they did, and she always did seem to have a lot of money to spend. Her father came here to work at one of the observatories. He's really into astronomy, has a pile of degrees. Her mother likes to do the social scene, and there isn't much of one there in Hilo so she flies over to Honolulu all the time. I'm sure Crystal got her to cover the airfares for Stacey, Allison, and Cathy."

"Why did Crystal live with you girls? I take it the others are more like you than her?" Greg had seemed genuinely puzzled.

"Yep. The rest of us are just regular people. Stacey is the only one from the mainland other than Crystal, and her folks sound like ordinary people too." Kim had to laugh at the description. "Crystal had already been living in Hilo for a while and actually graduated from a local high school. She always said she wanted to experience a regular college life."

"I'm surprised she didn't go to a school on the mainland."

"I always felt that way too." Kim grinned. "I could really see her at a school in California, especially as a sorority girl."

"Oh, yeah," Greg had agreed. He'd met a few sorority girls from the mainland and everything he heard about Crystal put her in the same category.

Kim, meanwhile, had turned philosophical.

"I finally decided that while Crystal puts on a good front, inside she's basically a frightened little girl. I don't think she wants to be too far away from Mommy and Daddy. Maybe Daddy more than Mommy, because he was always there when she needed something. And I also think she liked being a big fish in a small pond there at the university in Hilo."

"Makes sense. I can't wait to meet her. It's an interesting combination, femme fatale and Daddy's little girl."

Kim had made a noncommittal noise in her throat. The idea of Crystal and Greg meeting still made her nervous. Maybe she herself wasn't the mature woman she pretended to be, either.

"So why is your entire weekend taken up? You only mentioned picking up the dress on Monday."

"Julie is the matron of honor—she's the one who got married last June . . ."

"Ah . . ."

"Yes. The unfortunate event." Kim had frowned. She really needed to get beyond that. She was able to talk about it, but when it came right down to it, she didn't want to. It was easier with Greg, though.

"Julie decided this would be the perfect time to have the bridal shower, since the three out-of-town girls will be here. That's on Saturday afternoon. Then we'll spend the night and all go to brunch on Sunday. The out-of-town people will be staying over for the fittings on Monday, of course, but I plan to come home. I'm sure Julie will go home too. She's spending Saturday night, and she's still a newly-wed, so I'm sure she won't spend Sunday too."

She could hear Greg's soft laughter. "I think you're right."

Then his had tone shifted, his voice filled with concern. "Will it be very difficult for you?"

"No." Kim had spoken instantly, even though she was far from certain. But she didn't want to admit that she might still care. She had her pride, and she would show them all that she was just fine, thank you very much.

And when they saw her with Greg at the reception, they would know it.

"Mom thinks I'm making too much of it, trying to show them how unaffected I am. But it's important to me. I don't want Crystal to gloat over stealing Henry. So I have to *show* her that I don't care."

"I think you're nuts."

"What?" The word had exploded from her mouth before she'd even had a moment to think. How could he say that?

"You should have declined politely when she invited you to be a bridesmaid, Kim. You still could have gone to the wedding and taken a date and shown her you didn't care."

It sounded so reasonable when he said it. But she hadn't taken the time to be thoughtful and reasonable back when Crystal had first called. Back when she was still hurting from Henry's desertion. *Pride goeth before a fall*, after all.

Kim sighed. "Well, it's too late now. But even if I wasn't in the wedding party, I would have gone to the bridal shower, you know. There will be a lot of our mutual friends from college there, and I'm looking forward to catching up with all of them."

Greg didn't say anything for a moment. "Well, I'm sure it will be nice for you to see your old friends."

He paused for several heartbeats, and Kim had almost wished him good night: She was glad she'd remained silent when he spoke again. His voice was soft and deeply reassuring.

"You can call me anytime. Okay?"

Kim was so touched, she'd felt tears spring to her eyes. "Yes. Thank you."

She almost laughed when her final words registered. Now she was thanking him. That was good. She really had to balance their account soon, and this had been a step forward.

As she drove into Hilo, Kim tried to concentrate on all the old friends she would be seeing that afternoon. Julie said the response had been good to her shower invitations. Still, Kim had made sure she packed her aspirin—the new type made especially for tension headaches.

For the hundredth time, she reminded herself of the old friends she was likely to see at the shower. Stacey would be coming all the way from Seattle. It had been well over a year since any of them had seen her, since she had not come for Julie's wedding. Allison and Cathy were both flying in from Honolulu. Even Julie, who lived nearby in Waimea, wasn't someone she saw on a regular basis anymore. With all the old friends together again, she doubted they would get much sleep.

It really might be fun. There would be others there, too, friends who had not lived with them but whom they had socialized with. She looked forward to seeing all her old friends—except for Crystal. No matter how she tried to tell herself it wasn't entirely her old roommate's fault, Kim could not erase the tension she felt whenever Crystal was around. And even though she was relieved that she would not be spending the rest of her life with Henry, the way he'd jilted her was still a sore point.

Maybe she would be able to avoid Crystal, since the other four would be there too. With new hope, Kim turned onto the street leading to Crystal's house.

By the time Crystal got around to opening her gifts, Kim was beginning to relax. Things were going well. It really was great to see everyone again.

It wasn't until the rest of the guests had left that her friends finally turned to her and inquired about her life beyond family and career. And, of course, it started with Crystal.

"So, Kim," Crystal said. "You still haven't told us about this new boyfriend of yours."

They were lounging on the floor of the family room, sleeping bags spread out and ready. Crystal's comment drew exclamations from the others.

"A new boyfriend?"

"Is it serious?"

Although they had been close in college, real life had since intruded. Julie was newly married and busy with her husband and setting up their home. The other three lived far away. These days they seemed to see one another only at classmates' weddings. And while the still-single women moaned over how many of their classmates were getting married, that only amounted to once or twice a year.

"Tell, tell," Allison cried. "Is he wonderful?"

Kim couldn't get mad at her for wanting to know. Allison was inevitably happy and always smiling, with a personality that made everyone like her and want to smile back.

But Kim wasn't ready to tell. Deep inside, she was terrified that something would happen at the last minute and Greg would change his mind about accompanying her. After all, there were almost two months between Christmas, when he'd agreed to escort her, and the Valentine's Day wedding. Even now, almost a month remained for something to go wrong.

Besides, she was enjoying Crystal's frustration at not knowing. And she was sure the others would understand if they knew the whole story. Come to think of it, she thought, they *did* know the whole story. Just not the part about Greg.

"Well, I have been seeing someone," she said reluctantly. "I'm bringing him to the wedding. But for now it's so new and wonderful I just don't want to share."

Oops, wrong choice of words. She noticed Stacey wince, and glanced quickly at Crystal. But Crystal didn't react at all, though her smile began to look brittle.

"Can't you even tell us his name? What am I supposed to put on the placecard?" Crystal asked.

" 'Kim's date,' " Allison said, laughing. The others all joined in.

"I sure wish I would meet someone," Cathy said. She wrapped her arms around her drawn-up legs and rested her chin on her knees. "I'm beginning to feel as if I'm the only person in the world who doesn't have a significant other." She ended with a deep sigh that made the others laugh again.

"Don't worry," Allison told her. "There's someone out there for you. You just haven't met him yet."

"You wouldn't understand." Cathy frowned at Allison, sending a pointed look toward the other woman's left hand. "You have a fiancé."

The others all turned toward Allison.

"Have you set a date yet?" Stacey asked.

Allison shook her head, and Kim breathed a quiet sigh of relief. The others were drawn in by Allison's talk of her fiancé's reluctance to set a date. This was a much better topic for them tonight. With Crystal's wedding imminent, weddings were the topic of choice.

As Allison assured them they would all be bridesmaids for her and began to talk about colors and themes, Kim sank back into the shadows. This was harder than she'd thought. After all, she was the one who should be walking down the aisle next month, not Crystal. She and Henry might not have been engaged, but they had planned to marry and had even talked about a Valentine's Day wedding. Having him walk out on her had been bad enough—hearing the date he planned to wed Crystal had seemed like a second betrayal.

For the next hour, Kim stayed in her corner, safe in the shadows, listening to her friends talk about the men in their lives. She didn't know if they were respecting her wish to keep her own life private, or if they just forgot she was there; whichever it was, she was glad.

She was almost nodding off when Julie suggested popcorn, and everyone rose and headed for the kitchen. Kim was reluctantly shedding the cocoon of her sleeping bag to follow them when Crystal sank down beside her. Kim looked over at her but didn't say anything.

"I just wanted to thank you for coming," Crystal said. "And for the bread pans."

"You're welcome." Kim couldn't help thinking there was more to it than that. The heart-shaped bread pans she'd chosen were insignificant compared to most of the other shower gifts Crystal had received. Kim's mind worked overtime trying to figure out what Crystal might want. Unable to come up with a feasible answer, she tried to deflect her with a compliment.

"It's going to be the most beautiful wedding ever," Kim said sincerely.

There was no doubt at all that everything would be lovely. Crystal was a perfectionist who would not allow anything else. And she'd told them from the beginning that her parents were ready to mortgage their house to get her the wedding she'd always wanted. They all knew that would hardly be necessary, but Crystal thought she was just being "one of the girls" when she made statements like that.

"Thank you. I sure hope so." Crystal smiled as she accepted the compliment. Then she laid her hand on Kim's arm. "It's really great the way you're being so nice about everything, Kim. I didn't think you'd agree to be one of my bridesmaids. And I'm so glad you did. It just wouldn't be the same without you."

Kim almost felt a tear in her eye. Almost. Crystal sounded very sincere, but Kim remembered that she was an excellent actress who'd been involved in theater while they were at school. Still, she appreciated the effort Crystal was making and answered accordingly.

"We're friends of long standing, Crystal. I couldn't let a man ruin that."

A sting of guilt hit her as she said it. She *was* letting Henry ruin their friendship, though it had always been a fragile one. The only thing she and Crystal would ever have in common were their shared years at college.

Kim attempted to redeem herself by forcing a deprecating laugh. "But don't invite me to any intimate dinners once you're married, okay?"

"Okay." Crystal laughed as well. "Girls' night only."

They sat for a moment in silence, Kim wondering once again what Crystal really wanted.

"So, do you think this is it for you?" Crystal asked. "This new boyfriend, I mean? Your secret beau?"

Kim sighed. She should have known that Crystal was leading up to more prying about Greg. She let her frustration show.

"Honestly, Crystal, it's not exactly a secret. Everyone knows we're seeing each other." Well, sort of. Everyone in Malino thought they were a couple—except Kim and Greg themselves.

"So why won't you tell me who he is?"

Kim almost smiled. It was killing Crystal not to know

the name of her date for the wedding. And Kim couldn't help enjoying it, even though it made her feel guilty. But Crystal had stolen her almost-fiancé. Kim was almost certain Henry had to shoulder most of the blame, but it did take two to make a couple. Crystal could have refused to date him.

But Kim didn't want to gloat. She managed to keep her voice controlled, almost contrite, and her gaze lowered to her lap. And she spoke the truth. "I guess I'm just a bit superstitious about it, that's all. I'm afraid if I talk about him too much something awful will happen to cause a problem between us."

Crystal didn't say anything.

Kim started to rise, ready to join the others in the kitchen. The smell of popcorn was already filtering out to the family room.

Crystal, however, reached over and put her hand on Kim's arm, holding her in place. Her eyes sought out Kim's, giving her a beseeching look that she found hard to ignore.

"We didn't plan to fall in love," Crystal said. "It just happens like that sometimes."

Kim stared at her. She wanted to shake her arm free, to dislodge Crystal's hand. Yet she held herself steady, taking it like a penance.

"I'm so glad you have someone else," Crystal went on. "I was really worried at first, concerned that we'd hurt you. I just cried and cried for the first few days. It was awful. I was so happy about meeting Henry, and so upset about him breaking up with you."

Kim could hardly breathe. Crystal's regret sounded so genuine. "Crystal . . ."

"No, let me finish. This isn't easy. But I want to say it." She took a deep breath. "You're a true friend, Kim. To be so understanding. Because Henry told me that you two were talking about marriage. I know you told everyone it wasn't serious between you, but I do know better. And I'm so sorry."

"Crystal . . ."

"I really love him, Kim. I really do. And he loves me. And we both love you. I wish we'd met any other way, any other time."

Kim heard her swallow hard, but then the others were crowding back into the room.

Crystal jumped up and rushed from the room, mumbling something about the restroom.

Kim smiled automatically at the others, taking a handful of warm popcorn. But Crystal's heartfelt apology rang in her ears, and guilt clogged her chest. Crystal always had been dramatic—or perhaps melodramatic would be the more appropriate word. But the veneer of sophistication she usually wore had disappeared during their brief tête-à-tête, and that made her apology all the more real.

Kim accepted a soda from Allison and gulped down a mouthful. She didn't know if the dry popcorn had caused that tight sensation in her throat, or if it was her guilt at being unable to forgive Crystal.

The fizzy cola exploded into her throat and flew up into her nasal passages, making her choke and gasp and cough. A righteous punishment for her unforgiving thoughts, she wondered?

Kim managed to survive the evening with her old roommates, and brunch with them on Sunday morning.

Brunch was actually the best part of the weekend for Kim. They went to their old hangout, a slightly seedy chop suey house that hadn't changed at all since the days they'd gone there for cheap, plentiful meals. They were sad to learn that the owner had turned things over to his son after suffering a heart attack, though the son assured them his father was healthy again and enjoying his retirement. They ended up talking about old times throughout the meal. To her intense relief, there were no more private moments with Crystal.

As she drove home, Kim had to admit that she'd enjoyed seeing everyone. Well, almost everyone. She still didn't know what to make of Crystal's apology. And the fact that she couldn't get beyond her bitterness bothered her more than ever.

It was mid-afternoon when she let herself into the kitchen at home, just in time to hear the phone ring. She watched her mother pick it up, then hold it out toward her. Paula mouthed "Greg" at her just as Kim heard his voice in her ear.

"So, how'd it go?"

"What?" How on earth could he have known she'd just arrived back? She was so surprised to hear his voice, so shocked at his perfect timing, that his words didn't register.

"You were meeting with the old roommates, right?"

"Right."

A warm feeling spread through her. Having friends was so special. She'd missed this kind of closeness since Emma's baby was born. She still considered Emma her best friend, but since Devin's birth, Emma was just too busy being a mother for spur-of-the-moment phone calls and keeping up with the everyday happenings of her adult friends. So Greg's attentions felt very special.

"And you spent time with the bride?"

"Yes."

"So," he said, repeating his original question, "how'd it go?"

This time she got it. The warmth of friendship spread through her at this sign of his concern for her. "It was okay. I liked seeing my old friends and catching up on their lives. It's such a shame that we don't keep in touch more often. Everyone is so busy."

"That's just the way life is, Kim," Greg said.

"Yes, I know." She sighed.

"Crystal managed to get me alone—she wanted to apologize."

"That's good, right?"

Kim sighed again. "I don't know. I guess it's good. She sounded so sincere, but I kept remembering that she liked theater and was a good actress. And she was always kind of melodramatic about simple things—like seeing a spider or running into an old boyfriend."

"Do you think she was just putting on an act for the benefit of the others?"

"No. It wasn't that." Kim's voice turned thoughtful. "She waited until we were alone."

Just then, Paula motioned that she needed to start the blender, so Kim took the phone into the other room. She dropped into an overstuffed chair and leaned her head against the pillowed support.

This was better. She didn't want her mother overhearing everything she said.

"She cried, Greg. I felt terrible."

"Because you're not ready to forgive her and you feel guilty?"

Kim sucked in her breath at his grave voice. She could also feel her cheeks reddening at his perspicacity. "Do you read everyone's mind, or just mine?"

Greg laughed. "You've been scolding yourself about this ever since you first told me about it. And now you feel guiltier than ever because you wanted the bride to be what you consider her usual irritating self, and then she surprised you by apologizing."

"Oh, boy." Kim felt a sudden urge to cry. Her voice lowered until it was no more than a whisper. "How can you know me so well?"

"I'm your friend."

His statement was so simple, so sincere, Kim felt warmth flood her soul. Perhaps it was her cold heart, melting toward Crystal and Henry. "Thank you."

"No thanks needed."

It was Kim's turn to laugh as she swiped at a few tears that had managed to leak past her eyelashes.

"That's what I keep telling you, but it doesn't seem to make any difference. Maybe now we'll be even."

There was another short moment of silence. Kim realized that their phone conversations seemed punctuated by these moments, yet there was never an awkwardness to them.

"So you managed to get through the ordeal and survive."

She had to laugh again. "More or less." She twisted the phone cord through her fingers, staring at the curled cord as it stretched itself out. "They asked about you."

"They know about me?"

She could tell from the sound of his voice that it was his turn to be surprised. "Not really. But they know I'm bringing a date and Crystal is very curious." She laughed softly. "She said she needed to know your name for the placecards."

"Sounds logical."

"I guess. But I'm reluctant to tell her anything at this stage."

"Afraid she'll steal me away too?"

Kim laughed, even though she inwardly wailed that it was no laughing matter. And he was still reading her mind.

"No, I'm not afraid of that, because she won't get to

meet you until the reception, and she'll already be Mrs. Henry Leong by then."

"Ah, too late."

"You better believe it. No, I just want to show up with you on my arm and let them all drool."

"Drool?"

Was that incredulity she heard?

"Of course. You're a good-looking guy. You've got to know it. And if you don't, you're fooling yourself."

There was a pause at the other end of the line.

"I know I'm not ugly." His voice was cautious.

"I bet you don't have any trouble getting a date."

"On the contrary."

"I'm not talking about high school."

"Ahh . . ."

Kim thought for a moment. Greg had been a nerd in high school, but even that didn't mean that he couldn't get a date. It always had seemed easier for a plain guy to get a date than a plain girl.

"You don't have to say it, Kim." His voice held an ironic, self-mocking tone. "I know what I was. Still am, probably."

"Oh, now there you're wrong," she assured him. "You're a darn attractive guy, Greg. Take my word for it."

He was silent.

"What, don't you believe me?"

"Not really. I think you're just grateful because I'm rescuing you from going to this wedding alone."

Kim wondered if he was grinning. But his voice sounded pretty serious.

"Oh, I am. But I'm still not lying. You might be one of those guys who matures late." Kim blushed furiously. She couldn't believe she'd just said that.

"Did you get contacts?" she asked quickly.

"Actually, I had that laser surgery for near-sighted people."

So that was it. Kim rushed on, not giving him time to think about her previous words.

"You probably work out too. Because you look terrific. I can't believe the co-eds in Honolulu didn't chase after you."

Too late Kim remembered the rumors of his breakup with a woman just before he moved back home. She breathed a sigh of relief when her comment didn't provoke a melancholy reaction. His tone remained light.

"Oh, there were a few. But I don't think they were interested in me as a person. I think there are just a few women out there who feel incomplete without a man on their arm and a date every weekend."

"Boy, you really need some work done on your self-esteem."

His soft laughter made the hair on the back of her arms stand straight up.

"Ever heard of the pot calling the kettle black?"

"Oh, you're impossible." But she was laughing.

Greg basked in the sound of Kim's laughter. There was something about the sound of it that made him feel happy. And that was good, especially after she'd managed to dredge up his past with Teri. Pretty, sophisticated, city-bred Teri, who had dazzled him with her interest in a simple country boy. It wasn't until she'd told him her thoughts on his move back to Malino that he'd realized she'd been using him. Teri wanted to be the wife of a professional man. She wanted a comfortable life and a place in the social scene. And she knew she could only have that if her husband lived in Honolulu. When he decided to return home and turned down the job offer in Kailua, she lost her temper and accused him of leading her on, screaming about "wasting" a whole year with him.

Greg shook himself free of disheartening thoughts of Teri. He didn't want to remember her or the harm she had caused; she'd hurt not only him, but his dying mother as well with her treatment of her only son.

Greg directed his attention back to the telephone and the woman at the other end of the line. He liked the happiness that filled him when he was talking to Kim, the way she could make him laugh and forget past hurts. But he knew she would not be truly happy herself until she worked through her feelings about Crystal and Henry.

"So, what are you going to do about Crystal?"

He heard her sigh.

"I wish I knew."

"Do you have any more of these pre-wedding bridesmaid duties to do?"

"You mean besides picking up our dresses on Monday?"

"Yeah."

"Just the bachelorette party. That won't be until the Saturday before the wedding."

"Do you think you'll be okay on Monday?"

"Sure."

Greg listened to her prompt reply, but knew she was answering automatically, without thinking. So he waited, hoping she would consider for a moment how she might improve the situation the next time she was with Crystal.

When she didn't speak, he did.

"It was pretty nice of her to say something to you. It must not have been easy."

"No," Kim admitted. "She thanked me for being so understanding."

Greg nodded, even though he knew she couldn't see the motion. He thought Crystal was trying hard to mend things.

"Have you considered that she isn't the awful person you think she is? That what happened really was out of her control?"

Kim sighed. "That's what I've been wondering."

Greg heard what sounded like a hiccup, and he wondered if Kim might be crying.

"Kim . . ." he began.

"Oh, Greg, she went on and on about how she knows we were more serious than I let on to the others, and she's so grateful that I'll be in her wedding, and how upset she was right after it happened."

This time he heard her sniffle, and he was sure she was crying. Greg felt terrible for upsetting her, but he also knew that she needed to come to grips with her feelings before the wedding day.

"That sounds sincere," he finally said.

"It did, darn it." Kim paused. "I wanted to hate her. We were never the best of friends, so it wasn't hard to hate her. Hating her felt good."

Greg laughed because he could tell that her mood was changing. But there was something that had always bothered him about the whole situation.

"Why is it that you don't hate Henry?"

Greg's hand tightened on the phone as he waited for her answer. Was it because she still loved him?

"Oh, I do. Did."

She stopped, apparently trying to sort out her priorities. "I had enough for both of them."

Greg released his breath, hardly aware that he'd been holding it in while he awaited her answer.

"You're forcing me to think here, Greg, and I guess I haven't wanted to. But the truth of the matter is that I wanted to blame Crystal more than Henry. After all, if it was all her fault, then he didn't leave me because I didn't have what he needed."

Her voice grew so soft he could barely make out the words.

"I was so afraid there was something terribly lacking in me that I couldn't hold on to a man."

She laughed, but it was not a pretty sound.

"Kim." He spoke slowly, putting as much feeling as possible into his voice. "You are a beautiful, vibrant woman. Don't you ever think that there's anything missing in you, do you hear?"

He heard a sigh, then soft laughter.

"Are you sure you aren't a shrink, Dr. Yamamoto?"

It was his turn to laugh. "I'm sure."

"I always feel better after I talk to you, you know that?"

"I didn't. But I'm glad."

He smiled as he said goodbye and hung up the phone. Talking to her always made him feel better too.

Back at the Ascension home, Kim smiled as well. Greg was forcing her to work things out, and she was sure it would help rid her of the guilt and heaviness of heart she'd been carrying around these past six months.

Then her smile widened as she realized something else. He hadn't thanked her—not even once. But she had thanked him—twice.

Chapter Seven

Kim had a restless night, but she awoke bright and early Monday morning anyway. The bridesmaids had to be there precisely at nine-thirty when Lokelani's opened, as Stacey had to get a plane at noon; she was expected back at work in Seattle on Tuesday. As it was, she'd have to get most of her sleep on the plane. The whole wedding party would try on their dresses so Crystal could view the entire group together and see if they fulfilled her vision.

Kim talked to herself all the way to Hilo. Her tired brain pulled up whatever she could remember of Psych 101 as she tried to work out the relationship between herself, Henry, and Crystal. During the hour or so she spent in the car, she was determined to find a way to make things right with Crystal. Or at least not let herself feel so bitter toward the happy couple.

She tried to remember every one of Crystal's good qualities; then she recalled all of Henry's good and bad points, trying to see if one group would outweigh the other. She'd realized months ago that she and Henry would never have worked out well together. But she forced herself to be brutal. He was a nice man, and good-looking, and they'd had fun together. But he'd always been impulsive, and he had a temper, although it wasn't volatile.

She let her mind wander back to their first meeting. Her cousin Eddie had brought him to the Malino Christmas party a year ago. He'd told Henry all about Malino and their wonderful party, and when Henry claimed it was too good to be true, Eddie invited him to attend. Eddie introduced Henry to Kim and he'd left with her phone number in his pocket. Amidst her troubled thoughts, Kim had to smile at the irony; now she'd re-met Greg at the town Christmas party.

Kim and Henry spent a lot of time together in the six months following their meeting. Interestingly enough, she and Henry had much more in common than she and Crystal ever had. They both loved the ocean, swimming, and being outdoors. They went snorkeling, spear fishing, and canoe paddling.

Most of all, they'd both been proud of their Hawaiian heritage—the rich mix of cultural backgrounds that prevailed in modern-day Hawaii. They used to spend hours discussing the cultural heritage they would pass along to their children—a unique mix of Asian, Polynesian, and Caucasian. Kim couldn't help wondering how Henry felt now, as he prepared to marry a rich *haole* like Crystal, knowing his children would be predominantly Caucasian.

By the time she pulled into the parking lot across from Lokelani's, Kim felt ready to face Crystal. She took a deep breath and let it out slowly. Once again she visualized their undergraduate days of easy camaraderie. One last time she reminded herself how certain she was that marriage to Henry would have been a disaster.

Then she opened the car door and stepped outside, smiling at the others already gathered there. For the first time since June, she felt that the smile she offered Crystal was genuine. Crystal seemed to notice, too. Her expression softened as she returned Kim's greeting, and she gave her an impulsive hug.

Once inside, however, Kim had to grit her teeth and bite her tongue.

Crystal waited while her bridesmaids crowded into the changing area first to don their dresses. Then, although she admired them all lavishly, she also made critical remarks disguised as questions.

"Shouldn't this seam lie just across here?"

"Is Allison's neckline lower than Kim's?"

Kim wondered how the owner could stand it. But Dana Vieira, apparently used to picky clients, was singularly unaffected. She remained smiling and cheerful as she assured Crystal that she would take care of tiny imperfections that Kim couldn't even see.

Kim reminded herself that Crystal was a nervous bride. Then she thought of Henry and decided Crystal had every right to be nervous. Fighting an inappropriate giggle, Kim turned her attention back to Crystal, who was just emerging from behind the dressing room curtain.

There was a collective gasp of admiration. Even Dana seemed momentarily stunned before she stepped forward to adjust Crystal's train.

"Oh, Crystal. Wait till Henry sees you." Julie swiped at a tear as she said it.

Kim blinked back a tear herself. She could honestly admire the gown on Crystal and, stunning though it was, not feel a moment of yearning to have it for herself. Now that lovely white satin *holoku* displayed in the shop window, or the cream silk with the lace overlay that was reminiscent of a woman in an Erte print—those Kim could drool over.

Crystal's gown was a fairytale vision of a dress, the kind

of creation that might be featured on the cover of *Bride* magazine. Yards and yards of costly silk and lace, frothy tulle billowing out like a cloud. The strapless top hugged her torso to just below her waist, the entire bodice covered with lace and encrusted with pearls and crystal beads. The skirt was a sea of tulle trimmed with a scattering of more lace, pearls, and beads. Crystal looked absolutely gorgeous.

Kim gazed at her in the lovely gown and felt not an ounce of envy. She smiled broadly at Crystal's mother, who moved forward to make some small adjustment to the veil. Then she joined the bridesmaids in raving over Crystal and exclaiming what a beautiful bride she would be.

A full ten minutes were lost in exclamations of one sort or another, then the women lined up together before the wide mirrors. Crystal's mother passed out silk flowers of the type they'd ordered for the bouquets, so that they could see just how everyone would look.

There was a general sigh of pleasure. They made a pretty picture, the bride in her bouffant white, the attendants in slim, elegant chiffon dresses of a pale apricot, simultaneously both gold and pink.

Kim thought they looked wonderful, a feeling echoed by all the other bridesmaids. Crystal—a nervous bride, Kim reminded herself again—did not seem as pleased as the others, frowning at their reflection, making comments about hairstyles, and dictating nail polish hues. Her mother asked whether they would be wearing hose, then went on about pedicures and toenail polish.

At the end of the line, Kim and Allison exchanged winks and tried not to giggle. The more Crystal's mother found to question, the better Kim understood her daughter. The gowns were masterpieces, but both Crystal and her mother seemed determined to find problems.

Finally they announced themselves satisfied. The gowns

were put on hangers and inserted into protective covers, and everyone was able to leave. Saying her goodbyes to the out-of-towners, Kim felt genuine regret. But at least she could now look forward to the wedding, as she had not been able to do as recently as two days ago.

"Greg, you'll never guess."

Kim had gotten on the phone as soon as she and Paula finished dinner on Monday evening. She was anxious to share her morning with Greg, to let him know how much better she was coping. She would have called the moment she got home, but she remembered him saying that the clinic would be open, holiday or not.

"Ah, let me see."

His teasing voice made her feel deliciously frivolous.

"You let your jealousy get the upper hand and murdered the lovely Crystal this morning. You're calling from the county jail asking me to come bail you out."

"You're crazy, you know that?" Kim laughed. But she couldn't resist asking, "Would you? Come bail me out?"

"Aha! So you did do it. I can see the interviews now." He moved his voice up an octave so that it was high and squeaky. " 'She was such a nice girl. I never would have suspected it.' " His voice returned to normal. "That would be from your neighbor, of course."

"That's what you know," she retorted. "Mrs. Arruda would be much more likely to say that she 'knew all along there was something going on with that girl.' "

They both laughed.

Greg's voice turned serious. "But really, how was it?"

Kim couldn't curb her enthusiasm. "It was wonderful. I'm okay now, Greg, I really am. I looked at her in that gorgeous, hideously expensive dress and I wasn't the least bit jealous. I just kept reminding myself that I didn't want to marry Henry anyway. He and I have a lot of interests in common, but he's critical and impulsive, and would be very difficult to live with."

"Atta girl."

"And I have you to thank."

"What did I tell you about that?"

"I know, I know. I keep telling you the same."

She took a deep breath, feeling a peaceful calm settle over her. It was as comforting as Linus's blue blanket. "You and I are good for one another, Greg. Did you realize that yet?"

"Oh, yes."

Kim was so happy to hear his agreement that she didn't catch the fear in his voice.

Crystal and her perfect wedding were quickly forgotten as the town prepared for the Friday evening sunset wedding of Mele and Ben. This was a wedding of a completely different kind. Run on a shoestring budget, it was pulling together through the power of love and the cooperation of an entire town. It was *'ohana*—family—at its best. The whole town acted together as one enormous family.

Emma called Kim at the bank the following morning and suggested meeting for lunch.

"Devin is teething," she said, "and I was up most of the night with him. Matt or my mom will watch him while I get out for some sane time with another adult. If you can make it, that is."

"Are you kidding?" Kim jumped at the chance.

The chief topic of conversation, of course—once Emma told Kim all about Devin's latest developments—was the big wedding.

Kim supposed that she had Ben and Mele to thank for her renewed friendship with Greg, and she meant to find the most wonderful wedding gift she could afford. If she hadn't overheard Greg's comment that night of the Christmas party, the one about Ben's courage . . . if not for that, it might have been months before she'd ever seen Greg. After all, he'd been in town since the summer and she hadn't run into him once.

Because so many of the townspeople had helped Ben with his courtship, everyone was excited about the wedding. Mele's dress, sewn by Mrs. Young from the General Store, the mother of the matron of honor, was a popular topic among the women. The men wondered what kind of food would be served at the reception, and none of them was shy about offering suggestions. Everyone wanted to give their input.

It was impossible for Kim to avoid comparisons with Crystal's perfect wedding. She thought of Crystal's elaborate dress and her precise plans for every tiny detail.

"Crystal has made every decision herself," Kim told Emma, as they ate their sandwiches at the café near the bank, the same café where Mele had worked for so many years. "Sometimes I wonder if she's even consulted Henry."

Kim couldn't imagine Crystal's reaction if a friend or a neighbor had the temerity to suggest what she serve at her wedding reception. She hadn't even asked her old roommates how they felt about the style or color of their dresses.

"Pretty different, huh?" Emma said. She'd just finished telling Kim about the gift Mele's matron of honor was planning for her best friend. "It's so nice of Luana, don't you think? I doubt if Mele and Ben would be able to afford a honeymoon on their own."

"Oh, it's marvelous," Kim agreed. "I was just trying to imagine Crystal's reaction if someone told her they were giving her a stay at a resort for a wedding gift." Just the thought made her laugh. "She'd have a million questions about the place before she'd ever accept. If she did."

"Oh, and I forgot to tell you the best part," Emma said, her voice rising in excitement. "Luana's managed to track down a traveling canoe and it's going to pick them up at the park after the reception, and take them over to the beach in front of the resort to let them off. Mele said she has to have her suitcase sent over there beforehand."

Kim's eyes turned dreamy. "Leave it to Luana to do something like that. It's so romantic." She sighed in wonder. "You and Mele both have such romantic guys, too. How'd you get so lucky?"

"What's so romantic?"

The gruff voice startled the women, who had not heard Mr. Jardine approach their table. Kim explained her comment about the men, and they both told him the latest news about the Pitman-Mendoza nuptials.

The old man's eyes sparkled. "The Kukui Wana'ao Resort lost a good person when Luana gave up that wedding coordinator job."

Kim checked her watch. "Oh, my gosh. Look at the time."

She pushed her chair back, thanking Emma for lunch at the same time she grabbed her purse. "You stay and have some dessert with Mr. Jardine. I have to get back to work. We're so short-handed these days."

Kim started from the café, but Emma called out and came rushing after her.

"Wait."

They paused just inside the door, Kim unable to hide her curiosity.

"I just wanted to tell you . . ." Emma smiled broadly. "I couldn't help noticing that you're much more your old self today. Did you finally let go of that bitterness for what Henry did to you?"

Kim was speechless, which just made Emma laugh.

"Yep, I thought so. I'm really happy for you, Kim. Now you can enjoy the wedding on Friday, and your old friends on Valentine's Day as well."

She gave her a quick hug, then hurried back to the table where Mr. Jardine was perusing the menu.

Kim might have stared after her for another five minutes, stupid with surprise, if she hadn't been expected back at the bank.

Excitement tinged the air in Malino for the rest of the week. Mele and Ben's wedding was on Friday evening, and it was all anyone could think about. Every client who came into the clinic mentioned it; everyone Greg encountered on the street brought it up.

Aunty Deni readied the children's choir, who would sing *Kei Kali Nei Au*, the Hawaiian Wedding Song. Mrs. Young had already made all the dresses, but was sent back to her sewing machine in a panic when Kayla, one of the junior bridesmaids, managed to rip out the hem of her dress while showing it off to her friends.

Greg found it impossible to escape talk of weddings. Dresses, cakes, music, food for the reception—it was all anyone, male or female, wanted to talk about. His mother would have loved it.

By the time Greg stopped in at the bank on Thursday afternoon, he was more than ready to escape. So when he suggested dinner in Kona to Kim, he had to laugh at the way she accepted with such unsuitable haste.

"Getting tired of weddings too, are you?"

She nodded with seeming relief. "Does this mean we don't have to mention the word 'wedding' tonight?"

"Whatever you want," he agreed.

But privately, he was more than relieved. In fact, Greg found himself seriously conflicted by his feelings for Kim. He liked being with her. He liked talking to her on the telephone. He always felt happier afterward, as though she'd allowed a fresh breeze to blow through, cleaning out his life.

The whole thing was making him think too much about what it would be like to have her around all the time. And, with all the talk about weddings, it was getting so that a wedding was all he could think about as well. And that made him very unhappy. His losses were still too fresh.

Every day he watched his father and his grandmother try to get through another day. He could tell whenever they thought of his mother. A look would fill their faces, a softening of the expression. Then the realization would come that she was gone, and a look of pure devastation would replace that other, hopeful one.

And then he'd remember Teri, and how much he'd loved her. At least, he thought he had. Then he was devastated when he realized that the woman he loved didn't even exist. He'd created a version of Teri in his mind that was nothing like the real flesh-and-blood woman—the woman who appeared with a vengeance when he decided to follow his heart and not her desires. How could he trust his judgment about women after that disaster?

Every time Greg thought of how nice it would be to have Kim with him all day, every day, he would remember how wrong he'd been about Teri. How hurt he'd been when she left him with bitter words and not an ounce of regret.

And, he'd think about the devastation his father felt after losing the woman he loved. He might be an emotional coward, but did he want to open himself up for that kind of hurt? And what if something happened to *him*, and *she* was the one left devastated?

Greg found his mind too active these days, sleep harder to come by. He hoped that seeing Kim, getting away from Malino, would help him clear up some of his questions. At the least, he hoped it would help him relax and enjoy himself.

As they drove in to Kona that evening, Greg mentioned again the asperity with which she'd accepted his invitation.

"I was flattered at how happy you were to accept my invitation. And how quick."

Kim could hear the laughter in his voice, and had to grin as well.

"The thought of getting away from Malino for the evening was impossible to resist. You realize that tomorrow is the wedding. If I was home right now, I'm sure I'd be taking one call after another about some aspect or other of the wedding. I like Mele a lot—Ben, too—but enough is enough. Especially with Crystal's wedding coming up next month, I've really had about all the wedding talk I can stand."

Greg laughed. "Shall we just say that weddings are off-limits as a topic for the evening?"

"Oh, yes."

"But first, let me ask you this. Would you and your mom like to go to the wedding tomorrow with my family?"

Kim turned to him, a wide smile on her face.

"Oh, Greg, that would really be nice. I'm sure Mom will enjoy going with your family. Thank you."

"Okay. That's settled, then. No more wedding talk," he declared.

They both laughed. Kim decided she liked to hear Greg laugh. His laughter had a deep throaty quality that seemed to infiltrate her system and allow her to feel his happiness. It wasn't something she'd ever noticed with any other person.

The thought of the evening ahead brought her such pleasure, it almost scared her.

They found many other topics of conversation that evening, staying out until quite late. As Kim pulled up her covers around midnight, she remembered again how much she'd looked forward to the evening. And, yes, she should have been frightened. Because she was fairly certain that she was falling in love with Greg Yamamoto.

Friday morning was clear and bright, the sun shining. The forecast promised the warmest day of the new year. The bank was busy as people ran in and out with periodic reports of decorating progress at the park.

Despite her complaints to Greg the previous evening, Kim was excited about the wedding, and anxious for all the news.

They arrived at the park early at the insistence of Paula and Violet, who wanted to get good seats. Kim didn't mind either, as she was anxious to see the results of the activity she'd heard about all day.

She was very happy to be off; Corinne had drawn the late shift at the bank this Friday evening and had been lamenting her bad luck ever since.

As soon as the ladies found some chairs, Frank and Greg moved off. Kim noticed that most of the women were seated while the men clustered to the sides talking. A quick look confirmed that there wouldn't be enough chairs for everyone, so the men would probably remain standing. After being on her feet most of the day, Kim appreciated the old-fashioned courtesy, even if it did smack of male chauvinism.

The day had lived up to its early promise. As evening approached, the temperature remained warm. The sky was a beautiful blue with a few fluffy white clouds too bright and high to threaten rain.

Kim listened to the women around her discussing the decorations as her gaze moved over the area. People from the church where Mele and Ben were active members had done it all. Chairs were arranged in rows with an aisle at the center for the bride.

At the front, an arch had been constructed from two-by-fours and covered with greenery and white flowers. Local gardens had probably been denuded, Kim thought, as she spent the time before the ceremony noting the various flowers that made it into a work of art. Gardenias, spider lilies, Singapore plumerias, roses, poinsettias, anthuriums and spathiphyllums, ginger, jasmine, hibiscus, tiare, and a plethora of orchids of various varieties filled every bit of space on the arch, curving over the top and plunging down the sides. It proved the perfect backdrop for the ceremony.

As the couple exchanged their vows, the setting sun dropped below the horizon and the sky turned into a pink and orange postcard of a Hawaiian sunset. The white flowers glowed in the dimming light, as did Mele's white *holoku* and Ben's traditional white shirt.

Kim wiped a tear from the corner of her eye as the Reverend Charles presented the newlywed couple to the crowd. At their sides stood the wedding party—as different from Crystal's perfect bridesmaids as it was possible to get. Beside Mele stood her best friend, Luana, and Mele's twin ten-year-old nieces. Beside Ben stood his brother and two ancient cowboys, the two ranch hands he'd inherited along with his great-uncle's land.

There was no expensive silk and lace wedding dress, no carefully tended private garden, no elegant little chamber music quintet. Mele and Ben stood up with the people who were important to them, in front of the people who made up their lives, with the sound of the surf in their ears and the smell of tropical flowers scenting the air. Kim couldn't imagine anything more appropriate. Anything more perfect.

Kim looked for Greg among the men, and their eyes met briefly as they cheered the new Mr. and Mrs. Mendoza. Kim smiled.

But Greg's eyes remained sober and troubled, and his gaze shifted away.

A week of cold wet weather followed, making the beautiful weather for Mele's wedding seem providential, as though a benevolent god had smiled down upon the union of Mele and Ben and upon the town of Malino.

The entire three weeks between Mele's wedding and Valentine's Day were wet and miserable. Day after day brought showers until the ground was wet and soggy.

On days without rain, it remained cloudy and gray, and snow on Mauna Kea made the air cold. Bank customers complained that mainland relatives refused to believe how cold it could get in the islands, and showed no sympathy whatsoever.

The weather brought illness, too. Every third person in Malino seemed to be ill with either a cold or the flu. Kim thought that she would scream if one more person coughed in her face while conducting bank business. They always apologized, and she could see how sorry they really were but it didn't help her fight off the germs that had already penetrated her air space.

Because of this, she wasn't surprised to awaken on Wednesday morning, ten days before Valentine's Day, to find that every muscle in her body ached. She'd finally gotten the darn flu. The only good thing to come of it was the pleasure of staying home in bed, just listening to the rain drum on the roof, instead of being out there in it. Unfortunately, she couldn't enjoy it too much, because it was impossible to make her achy body comfortable.

She had little appetite for dinner, but made an effort to consume the chicken soup her mother prepared. She'd just gotten back into bed when her mother came into her room and handed her the telephone.

"Here," she said, a wide smile on her face. "Maybe he can cheer you up."

"I heard you've got the flu."

A smile tickled its way to her lips. Talking to Greg really was a good way to brighten her day, even one as miserable as this.

"Good news travels fast."

She shifted around in bed, pushing herself up against the pillows in the hopes that it would make her feel more comfortable. Even the cats had deserted her, her constant movement as she sought a restful position finally chasing them away.

"Would you like me to bring you some chicken soup?"

"Thanks, but I just had some. My mom is taking care of me. She already had the flu last week, so I don't even have to worry about passing it along to her."

Then his words penetrated her brain and made her pause. "You can make chicken soup?"

"No." She heard his soft laughter. "But I warm up a mean can."

She could hear him chuckle and a soft laugh bubbled up in her own throat.

"Don't make me laugh. It hurts my chest."

"Sorry." He was instantly contrite.

"There's a good side to this, you know," Kim said.

"There is?"

"Yes. I'll be missing Crystal's bachelorette party." She paused as she readjusted her position yet again.

"Let me confess something—I'm relieved. Not that I'm happy to be so sick," she hastened to add. "And this flu is really miserable. But I'm not sorry that I'll miss the party. Even though I can look at Crystal now without wanting to claw her eyes out, I just wasn't really happy about one more party. I already called Julie and asked her to take in my gift for me."

"Ahhh. So you weren't looking forward to . . . uh, what do women do at those things?"

"What do men do at bachelor parties?"

She heard his soft laughter. "I think I better take the fifth on that."

"That bad, huh? Well, women aren't *that* bad. We go to a bar for drinks and give the bride naughty presents."

"Naughty presents?" He sounded intrigued. "Like what?"

"Sexy lingerie and stuff."

The conversation was making her uncomfortable, and she wriggled against the pillows trying to find a position that didn't make her ache even more.

"Stuff, huh?" Greg said. "Okay . . ."

"Nothing really bad," she insisted, wondering what he might be imagining. "Someone mentioned finding a deck of cards with nudes on the back. That kind of stuff. But I just wasn't in the mood."

"Too many weddings, huh?"

"I guess."

She couldn't possibly tell him that all this wedding talk was making her yearn for more from their relationship.

"I can sure understand that. I think every old lady in town has been at the clinic since Ben's wedding. Everybody saw us together, and the hints are coming fast and furious."

Kim was surprised. "But we were with our families."

"Yeah. I thought that would help, but apparently not."

Kim heard the depressed tone of his voice and felt worse than ever. Not only did she have the flu, but the man she was in love with was unhappy because everyone was trying to match them up.

She heaved a heavy sigh, which he promptly reacted to. "I'd better let you go. I'm sure you need lots of sleep."

"I've been sleeping most of the day."

"Still . . ."

He said a hasty goodbye and Kim wanted to cry. She wanted to spend her life with him, and he couldn't get away fast enough.

She remembered the somber look she'd caught when she'd searched out his eyes at Mele's wedding. What had happened? *I decide I'm in love with the guy, and suddenly he doesn't want to spend time with me?*

Kim flopped down lower into the blankets, wriggling into the bed until she'd formed a cocoon-like area of comfort. Then she closed her eyes and tried not to think of a life without Greg.

Chapter Eight

Valentine's Day finally arrived. Kim turned off the alarm, tumbled out of bed, and looked outside. The skies were heavy with gray, rain-filled clouds. Kim was torn between sympathy for Crystal and her hopes for a perfect wedding, and a guilt-inducing pleasure that the day might not be all Crystal had hoped for. As she told Greg in the car as they drove in to Hilo, "It's not that I don't want her to have a nice wedding. It's just that she made such a big deal out of having everything just perfect . . ."

"It might not be raining in Hilo," Greg reminded her. He'd borrowed his father's sedan for the trip, not wanting to take Kim to a formal wedding in his truck. But it made the trip more intimate, being together in the smaller car.

"Yeah, I thought of that too. And that would be really nice. But it does rain a lot in Hilo, something like a hundred and twenty-five inches a year. We all reminded her of that when she started making her plans."

Kim glanced out the window at the dripping trees. After weeks of rain, the often-dry creek beds at the roadside were filled with water, and small waterfalls appeared at intervals.

"I really thought she would opt to have it at one of the big resorts on the Kohala coast, where it's sunny most of the time." It was one of the more puzzling aspects of Crystal's wedding, her choosing to have the ceremony in a less than stellar locale. "But she said she loves the Pua Lani Gardens and that she and Henry go there all the time."

A visual of the beautiful grounds of the Pua Lani Gardens drifted through Kim's mind, but she found it hard not to picture it dripping with rain, the grass soggy, water or even mud seeping into their dyed apricot shoes. The picture brought her closer to giggles than to tears—which was probably a good thing.

"It does make you wonder though, doesn't it?" Kim turned to Greg, whose eyes remained focused on the road ahead. "Like there's a divine influence having a hand in things here, reminding us of who's running things."

Kim turned back to watching the damp landscape, wondering if the rain would continue all day.

"Did you know that old-time quilters used to make deliberate mistakes in their quilts, because they believed that only God was perfect? That's why you might see a photo of an old quilt and there will be a glaring irregularity in the design somewhere." She pursed her lips while she considered this practice. "I think it's rather odd, but at the same time there's something very special about it, you know what I mean?"

She felt flustered at not being able to communicate her thoughts in a more understandable manner, but it turned out it wasn't necessary.

"I do," Greg replied. "But do you mean to imply that Crystal was trying to play God by aiming for perfection, and so now it's raining so she'll understand that no human is perfect?"

Kim frowned. "It does sound silly when you spell it out

that way. And petty. But sometimes you just have to respect Mother Nature. Haven't you noticed how things can go wrong when you try to do something that seems against the natural order?"

It turned out that this was a pet peeve of Greg's, and they spent quite some time discussing DNA research, cloning, and other modern marvels of science.

Once that conversation played itself out, they watched the road and the rain and enjoyed a bit of silence. Until Greg interrupted with a question.

"Tell me again why we're driving in so early for a six o'clock wedding?"

Kim turned toward him immediately, her expression contrite. "Oh, Greg, I'm sorry. I told you you didn't have to drive me. We all have to be there early because of hair and nail appointments. Crystal's arranged to have someone come out to her house, can you imagine?"

Greg laughed. "Sounds fine to me. I don't know much about that stuff, I'm afraid. And I couldn't see us both driving in alone. Then you'd have to drive back alone tonight too, after all."

"Yeah, that wouldn't have been any fun. So, thanks. This is much better," Kim said.

"And wedding parties usually go to a hair and nail salon," she continued. "I never heard of having someone come to you. But it will be nice for us, I'm sure. Probably a lot of fun, too."

Kim looked out at a small lunch shop already doing a brisk business at eleven o'clock.

"I hope she has some lunch for us. I'm hungry."

She turned toward Greg. "What will you do while I'm busy getting ready?"

"Don't worry about me. I'll visit my Aunty Linda."

"Is that your father's sister?"

He nodded. "Yes. I haven't seen her since the funeral, so we have some catching up to do. I called her and she'll be home all day. In fact, she doesn't get out much since her husband died, and she wants me to take her shopping. I'll probably spend the day at Wal-Mart." He sent Kim a long-suffering look that merely made her laugh.

"What is it with guys and shopping?"

"We didn't get that gene," he responded. "I think we missed the primping one too. Will you really spend all afternoon getting ready?"

"Of course. We'll all be there together, so there will be a lot of talking. We'll have to take turns having our hair and nails done. And then there's makeup. I'm sure Crystal will have a lot of input about everything." Kim rolled her eyes.

"You'll do fine," Greg said. "Do you all tease the bride about the honeymoon?"

Kim shot him a questioning look. "What?"

"Forget it." Greg shrugged. "That's what guys do with the groom before a wedding. They tease him a lot about the honeymoon."

Kim decided to let that pass. If there was anything she preferred not to discuss—not even to think about—it was Crystal and Henry on their honeymoon.

Greg's day passed quickly once he arrived at his aunt's house. She was glad to see him, though he thought it had more to do with his driving ability than his sterling company. Aunty Linda was his father's older sister, who no longer drove due to problems with her eyes. So her ability to go out and about rested in the hands of others. He reminded himself of this as he carried bags and bags of groceries and dry goods into the house that afternoon.

Afterward, he felt the need for a shower before he donned the suit he'd brought to wear to the wedding.

The first thing he noticed as he was ushered into the wedding area at Pua Lani Gardens was the tent overhead. The rain had not been limited to the Kohala area. It had rained on and off throughout the day in Hilo, and Crystal's wedding was off to an imperfect start. But at least it would be dry.

Greg had arrived at the last possible moment, not wanting to wait around since he wouldn't know anyone. He'd no sooner taken his seat than the chamber group stopped playing and two ushers dragged a white carpet down the makeshift aisle.

Greg smiled. At least Kim wouldn't ruin her shoes. She'd spent several minutes lamenting that possibility in the car on the way in, moaning about the price of the dress and matching shoes, then facing the possibility of wrecking one or both.

Kim was the second woman down the aisle, and Greg couldn't take his eyes from her petite figure. She looked lovely. The gown wasn't the best color for her honey-brown skin, but the style was flattering and she held herself like a queen. He thought her smile seemed tight, and hoped she wasn't discomfited, imagining everyone speculating about her prior relationship with the groom. A futile hope, he imagined.

As she moved forward, he caught her eye and tried to smile some encouragement, but he wasn't sure he'd pulled it off. Watching her progress down the aisle made it impossible not to think of her as a bride herself. And not Henry's, either.

Greg swallowed hard as Kim pulled up adjacent to his row and sent him a bright smile. His gut twisted as he realized how important she'd become to him in the past few weeks. He didn't know how it had happened, and he was still fighting it. He couldn't forget Teri and his complete lack of judgment about her personality and motivation. Kim had been deeply in love with Henry, and look at how that had turned out.

Greg just couldn't stop thinking that love just naturally led to hurt, to loss, and to pain; and—coward though it made him—he didn't feel able to handle any more of that.

Butterflies fluttered in Kim's belly as she started down the long aisle with its sea of faces turned toward her. She tried to pretend that none of these people knew anything about her and Henry, when in truth probably everyone did. Was that whispering or just the murmur of the violin?

She straightened her spine and looked straight ahead. Henry stood there at the end of the aisle, waiting for his bride. To her surprise, his face turned red when she met his eyes, and he shifted his gaze to the floor. The death grip she had on her bouquet loosened.

Feeling somewhat better, Kim was able to smile and took another step forward. Greg's familiar face appeared at her left and she read the admiration in his eyes. Instantly, she felt better.

It was difficult, walking calmly, trying to pretend everything was okay. She was certain there was whispering following her down the aisle and felt sure it didn't have anything to do with her dress or hairstyle. Seeing Greg's encouraging smile was balm to her soul.

The ceremony proceeded without problems, the drizzle kept well away from the party beneath the tent. The sunset wasn't as glorious as the one Mele had had three weeks ago, and there was no soothing sound of surf. But even though the gardens were wet, they were still filled with blossoms and color, and the dampness did not prevent the perfume of hundreds of tropical flowers from sweetening the air.

As she followed the happy couple back up the aisle, Kim felt that, despite the weather, Crystal had managed a memorable wedding and one she could be proud of.

The reception that followed was equally impressive. To Kim's delight, Crystal had opted for the bridal couple to share a table for two at the front of the hall. Kim was thrilled, because it meant all the attendants were seated with their dates for the evening—the bridesmaids on one side of the head table and the groomsmen on the other. Poor Greg would not be alone in a sea of strangers; he sat right beside Kim, who introduced him to all her old friends. They had a great time. Kim thought that their table was the liveliest one there.

Kim wasn't surprised at the final seating arrangement. Crystal loved being the center of attention; why should she share her big day with her pretty friends? She almost felt sorry for her, though. While the bridesmaids' table talked and laughed and had a grand time, Crystal and Henry sat side by side, mostly in silence, broken by quick kisses as spoons clinked against glassware.

Kim found herself entering into the reception activities with a light heart. The ordeal was over. She was sitting beside Greg, eating good food, visiting with old friends. The world was a happy place.

She even made an attempt to catch the bouquet, which fell far short of the group awaiting it and landed on the floor at their feet. While they all stared at it in surprise, Allison grabbed it up, and Kim cheered with the others.

Greg made less of a try for the garter, standing at the very back of a group of unenthusiastic bachelors. That left the field open for a teenage boy, who leaped into the air to make the lucky catch. He blushed scarlet when he pushed the garter onto Allison's leg, but everyone could see he was proud as well.

In between the usual wedding reception activities, they danced. Kim learned that Greg was not an enthusiastic dancer, claiming two left feet. He did make an effort, but even she had to admit he was not especially talented on the dance floor. Still, they managed to have fun.

Finally, the deejay announced a very special event. The bridal couple would be leaving as their guests enjoyed a fireworks display over the gardens.

Everyone trooped outside, spirits high. Kim and Greg joined the other bridesmaids and their dates, huddling under umbrellas provided by the garden staff. Greg put his arm around Kim's shoulders and pulled her close, pushing aside the umbrella for a better view of the overhead show.

"What do you think?" he asked. "It's only a light sprinkle."

"My dress will be ruined," Kim muttered. She nestled her head into Greg's shoulder, leaning back against him and borrowing some of his masculine warmth. The rain had made it chilly outside.

Greg pulled the sides of his jacket forward, enclosing her in a cocoon of warmth. She was so slim, it wasn't too difficult to accomplish. He loved the way she snuggled into him.

"Do you mind if it's ruined?" Greg shared his earlier thought about the color of the dress doing little to enhance Kim's exotic beauty. "It would probably look good on Crystal," he added, almost whispering the words into her ear as they stood in their own little world among the larger crowd. "Pastels usually look good on blondes."

While she watched the explosions of color overhead, Kim considered Greg's idea. She liked the dress and the color, but she had always thought she looked better in bright jewel tones. "So you think she chose a color to enhance her own beauty rather than play up our strong points, huh?"

"Wouldn't surprise me."

Greg thought it rather selfish of the bride, but then, it was her day to shine. And everything he'd heard about Crystal led him to believe she would do exactly that.

"Red would have been a good choice for Valentine's Day, and all of you girls would have looked great in it. Why didn't you all wear red?"

Kim sighed. When she'd agreed to be a bridesmaid, she'd hoped for a red dress, one that she might be able to wear again for some future Christmas or Valentine's Day event.

Kim pressed her head into Greg's shoulder, loving the close contact and the quiet conversation that tickled at her earlobe.

"Too much of a cliché for Crystal," she said, as red twinkling lights exploded into giant chrysanthemums in the dark skies above.

"So . . ." Greg kept his eyes on the road, but his voice was so warm Kim felt as though they still stood wrapped in his jacket beneath the artificial stars. "How are you, really?"

"I'm okay. But I sure am glad it's over."

She saw his smile and couldn't resist one of her own. Because she really was okay. She'd dealt with Henry, who'd needed little handling because he'd spent the evening deliberately avoiding her; she'd managed to accept a private apology from his parents with dignity; and she'd kept her head high in front of her friends. Mostly, she'd stayed close to Greg and the other bridesmaids, and she'd had a very good time. And she no longer feared she would be seen as an object of pity, the poor girl who hadn't been able to hold on to her boyfriend.

Kim stared out the damp windshield. "The food was good, didn't you think?"

Greg laughed, and Kim ended up laughing with him. Okay, so changing the subject with talk of food was a cliché. But it worked quite well nonetheless. Wasn't that how things became clichés?

"The food was pretty good," Greg agreed. "You never know how it will be at these big shindigs. I really liked the cake."

She laughed. "Ah, the way to a man's heart. It must have been the coconut cream filling."

The two of them stared at the road ahead in silence for several minutes.

"Weddings really get you to thinking, don't they?" Greg said.

Kim made a sound in her throat that signified her agreement. It was followed by a lull during which she could almost hear Greg getting his thoughts in order. When he spoke, his voice was solemn and Kim knew this was something that was important to him.

"Do you think about your father, and how it will be on your wedding day without him?"

Kim took a deep breath in and released it slowly. She'd been right. This was important. Her voice was as solemn as his when she replied.

"Every time I go to a wedding."

Greg continued to stare straight ahead, but Kim could almost see his mind whirling.

"I was thinking about my mother today. Someday, I'll get married, and Mom won't be there."

Kim thought she heard a catch in his voice. She reached over, placing her left hand lightly on his arm. Was this what had caused that somber expression she'd noticed at Mele's wedding?

"It's not easy losing a parent. Some things are harder than others. When I graduated from college . . ."

This time her voice held a hitch. She drew her hand back, clasping it with her right hand and holding them tightly together in her lap. "I kept thinking how proud he would have been, seeing me walk across the stage in my cap and gown. He always said he wanted us all to go to college."

She stared out at the lights shining from the windows of the houses they passed. She was amazed that so many people were still up at this late hour.

"Weddings are the hardest time. Watching the bride walk up the aisle on the arm of her proud father . . ."

She watched another car approach from the opposite direction, its headlights blurring in the rain—or was it from the moisture in her eyes?

She waited until the car moved beyond them to speak again. "Holidays are hard too."

"I'll say. Christmas was awful. Dad tried so hard, but we all were missing Mom and we knew it was hardest on him."

"And people all try so hard to be nice because they want to help," Kim said. "But no one mentions his name because they think it's insensitive."

"Yeah, why is that?" Greg asked. "Everyone wants to help but no one ever talks about her. What would be nice is having people tell me how much they liked doing things with her, or how much she helped with the church flowers, or whatever." Kim could hear the frustration in his voice. "Instead, they all tiptoe around, afraid to mention her name. Like I'm going to break down and cry on their shoulders or something."

"That's exactly it," she said. "I think they are afraid that they'll make us cry."

"The mention of something she did that impacted their lives. That's what would be nice to hear," Greg said. "And I don't think it would bring tears. Not the overwhelming kind, anyway. Like the night you told me about the wreath she helped you make. That was a special moment for both of you, and I enjoyed sharing the memory with you. That's the kind of thing I'd like to remember. I'm sure there are a lot of other events like that that I don't even know about."

Kim thought about it for a moment.

"I guess I can understand that no one wants to talk about death, but it would be nice to hear memories of their lives." She patted his arm again. "It does get better though, I can tell you that. Now that it's been five years since Dad died, his old friends do talk about him. They reminisce about the good times, or laugh over something foolish they did together. It's nice to hear about his life from his friends."

"I guess I'll have that to look forward to." Greg's voice remained sad. "Eventually."

Greg wasn't surprised when he and Kim lapsed into silence after such an emotionally intense discussion. He'd noticed before that silences between them were comfortable, unlike similar situations he'd faced in the past with women he'd dated. Teri had been one of the worst, unable to sit through even two minutes of silence.

In fact, everything about being with Kim was comfortable. In the month and a half since they'd renewed their friendship, he'd found more and more that he counted on talking things over with her. He liked telling her about the little irritants that spoiled his days, about the ways he and his father clashed while living in the same house. She often confessed to similar problems with her mother, so they could sympathize with one another. And make one another feel better after talking it over together.

But they didn't just rehash life's aggravations. They also related the little fun things that made life sweet. He told her about the animals he saw at the clinic, about how the owners sometimes acted so out of character in their concern. She recounted gossip she heard at the bank, or tales her mother brought back from the medical center.

It had not yet been two months, yet their time together had been enjoyable in a way he hadn't felt for a long, long time. When he'd seen her stroll down the aisle that afternoon, his heart had done a strange flip. She looked so beautiful, easily outshining the bride, in his humble opinion. Even in the pale apricot dress she'd been lovely, a goddess of spring. They'd become friends, pure and simple, and it was good to have a friend.

But he was afraid their friendship might be heading toward something more, and he was uncertain about it.

He still had male friends from his high school days who lived in town. He'd renewed those acquaintances too, but many of them were married now. Some had children. They had other things to worry about, families to keep them busy. But he did go running with Keoni several times a week, and had stopped out at Russ's family's ranch to ride.

Russ was one of the old gang who had a family, and it did give Greg a warm feeling deep in his chest to see him with his small son. The little boy could even ride, his short chubby legs hugging the sides of his pony while he grinned at his father and his friend. There was a baby daughter too, and Russ beamed with pleasure when he talked about her. Mostly, he bragged that she was the prettiest, smartest baby ever to grace the island.

In his mind, Greg saw Kim again as she strolled down

the aisle, looking for all the world as pretty as a bride herself. He kept seeing her as a bride—as *his* bride—and it scared him. And warm thoughts of family and children scared him even more. He was a big, tall, strong man and he couldn't face the thought of love. He couldn't bear the hurt he foresaw if he'd called things wrong, couldn't bear another loss. What would he do if he gave his heart to Kim and she handed it back to him? It seemed that Teri had done more than hurt him. She'd undermined his confidence in his ability to read a person's character.

A fearful frown turned down the corners of his mouth, and he had to fight to maintain a neutral expression. He was disgusted with himself, and he didn't know what he should do. Forget about seeing Kim again? Even though he enjoyed being with her so much? Or forget about her or any other woman and become a bitter old man at the age of twenty-nine?

He needed to regain his self-confidence, but at the moment he had zero ideas of how to do it.

On the other side of the car, Kim snuggled into the seat, wishing she'd thought to change out of her bridesmaid's dress before they left the gardens. Formal dresses were often beautiful, but they were rarely comfortable. The flattering bias cut looked lovely when the wearer stood, but it bunched and pulled when she sat. The stiff label at the back neckline was beginning to irritate her skin. She wiggled, trying to relieve the itch it created at the center of her back.

She liked watching Greg drive. He relaxed into the task in a manner that showed confidence and ability. His hands gripped the wheel loosely, but she knew they would be able to control it if anything went wrong.

Kim liked Greg's hands. They were large, strong and capable. She could imagine him running them over a cat or a dog while he crooned soft nothings in the animal's ear. Those hands would be gentle, yet they would probe for hidden problems that might cause the creature discomfort.

Her eyes flicked up toward his face. Now and then, lights from oncoming traffic illuminated him briefly, brushing his features with harsh light. He had a strong face, and kind eyes. Greg inspired confidence, not the easiest task for such a young man. Yet she'd heard nothing but praise for him, and there did not appear to be any problems with clients changing over from old Dr. DeMello.

As his face was briefly illuminated, Kim was startled to see a fierce frown, quickly squashed. What on earth was he thinking of that would make him scowl that way?

Kim started to speak, but stopped when she saw the carefully neutral expression that Greg had adopted. Whatever he was thinking, it was private. Perhaps he was working something out.

Kim dropped her gaze back to Greg's hands. It remained there when she dropped off to sleep, imagining those strong capable hands running down a cat's spine, wondering what it would be like to feel them on her own.

Greg had to awaken Kim when he stopped in front of her house. She looked so pretty, so fragile, asleep in the corner of the car, he hated to disturb her. She also looked peaceful. Perhaps she really had gotten over Henry and his betrayal. He'd watched her carefully all night, and he hadn't noticed anything that indicated she might still care for Henry. To his great delight, she'd seemed entirely indifferent to her former boyfriend.

He examined her face again, thinking how innocent she looked, like a child, or an angel. Pushing back an urge to kiss her awake, Greg remembered Teri's lovely face. She could look angelic and beautiful too. Unfortunately, physical appearance was not enough.

Deciding he would need more time to work out his inner demons, Greg spoke softly.

"Kim. We're here."

Her lashes fluttered, but she didn't move.

Aw, the heck with it, he thought, moving his head closer. His lips met hers with a restraint he felt proud of. He touched feather-light kisses over her lips until she stirred, bringing her hand up to her mouth.

Her eyes blinked as she pulled herself from whatever dreamland she'd recently inhabited, and it took a moment for the faraway look in her eyes to switch to awareness.

"Oh!" She sat up, the seatbelt pulling at her shoulder, tugging the neckline of her dress dangerously low. "We're home."

Greg laughed. "Well, you are, anyway."

Kim managed to disengage the seatbelt and sit up. His words left her bereft. Their home should be together.

She ran her fingers through hair still stiff with styling gel and hairspray, trying to wake up more fully.

She leaned toward Greg. Had he really kissed her while she was dozing, or had she dreamt that? Her gaze settled on his lips with a look so longing he apparently recognized it for what it was.

With a groan, he pulled her into his arms and kissed her. This time there were no feather-light touches of the lips. His mouth pressed into hers, and she met his kiss with an eagerness of her own.

When they finally pulled apart, her lips felt swollen and her cheek stung from contact with his emerging beard. They stared at each other without saying a word. Kim was so in love, she wanted to shout it out. But she could see the emotions warring in Greg. It was obvious to her that he was fighting a spiraling attraction.

Kim struggled to find the right thing to say, then settled for the only think she could think of. It was far less than what she wanted to tell him, but she didn't want to push him toward a commitment he was not ready to make.

"Thank you for everything, Greg. It meant a lot to me, having you agree to be my date. I know guys aren't really into weddings. It must have been a sacrifice for you."

A soft smiled tipped her lips as she touched his suit coat. "You even had to dress up for it." Her hand brushed his lapel and softened to a caress that made them both suck in their breath. Kim pulled her hand back as though stung, just as Greg reached out to grasp it.

She clutched her hands together before her and almost stammered her next words.

"You look terrific in a suit. I saw all those women at the wedding giving you the eye." She smiled shyly.

Greg smiled back. She looked so good, so vulnerable. He wanted to believe that she was as sincere as she appeared to be. If only he could trust her, trust himself. Her pale dress glowed in the silver moonlight.

"Look." His voice was soft with wonder as he peered through the windshield. "It's stopped raining. There's a moon."

Kim leaned forward, a smile tilting her lips and charming him into stealing another kiss. He condemned himself for kissing her when he still felt unable to offer more than friendship. But he didn't feel bad enough to pull away until he remembered her previous comments about her neighbor.

"Do you think your neighbor is up at this hour?"

They both looked at the illuminated time display on the dashboard. It was almost one-thirty.

"I doubt it. But who knows? If she heard the car pull up . . ."

Their eyes met and they laughed.

"So," Greg said. "Want to give her something to see?"

Kim laughed, but she didn't protest when he kissed her again. But thoughts of Mrs. Arruda possibly spying on them gave Kim the giggles and they were soon out of the car and at the kitchen door.

Once all her things were set safely inside the door, Kim thanked Greg again. She had to grin as she realized how often she'd done it in the last few days. Maybe they were even now.

"So, I guess I'll be seeing you, huh?"

Greg looked startled at her words, and Kim kicked herself. She'd tried to choose her words so carefully. After those wonderful kisses . . . Still, he might be feeling trapped. She thought "I'll be seeing you" left things open-ended, in case he was afraid of commitment. And what she'd seen of him so far led her to believe he might be. But this evening brought the end of their agreement, so maybe he'd just as soon not see her again. Even after those wonderful kisses. She was so fully involved now, so in love, she was terrified of what might come next. Would he find someone else, like Henry? Like almost every other man she'd ever dated?

She didn't want him to think he had to keep seeing her. Yet what would she do if he didn't want to?

Greg continued to stare at her. He took hold of her shoulders and peered into her face, as though trying to read something there that she wasn't sure she wanted to reveal.

Could he see the love for him that she was trying so hard to control? She didn't think he was ready for that, and it might kill what they'd found together.

After what seemed a lifetime, Greg smiled. Relieved, Kim relaxed and smiled back.

"I see what you're doing," he said. Now his voice and his expression were suitably somber. "You're giving me a chance to back off, now that the wedding is past. But don't worry. Being your friend isn't a hardship. I like being your friend. I'd like to keep calling you, if it's all right. See what happens next."

If it's all right? See what happens next? Kim wanted to break into song. Maybe those old musicals had it right after all.

"Yes. It would be wonderful." Kim continued to smile up at him. Would he kiss her again?

"Okay then." Greg released her shoulders, but didn't move away from her. He stared into her eyes, trying hard to see into her very soul. She seemed like such a genuine person, but he no longer trusted his instincts about such things.

Kim stood quite still as he examined her, and he wondered if she was trying to read *his* mind. Her lips parted slightly as she looked into his face, and it was all the invitation he needed. With a groan low in his throat, Greg pulled her into his arms. He held her against his chest, struggling to keep his arms gentle and comforting when he longed to crush her to him. His pulse beat rapidly, but he could feel the thumping of her heart against his chest, and it rivaled his own.

Then his head came down, and he kissed her softly against her forehead. As Kim sighed lightly, he kissed her tenderly on her cheek. Kim squirmed against him, tilting her face in the hopes that he would find her lips.

But he had other plans. His lips rested quietly on her hair, then placed a delicate kiss on her ear. By the time he moved back to her cheek, he was laughing quietly. He needed to keep things playful, or he might succumb to heavier feelings and ruin anything they might have in the future.

But Kim wasn't feeling playful. With a decisive movement, she raised her hands, grasped his head, and planted her lips on his. His laughter stopped, caught in the emotion of the moment.

When they were done, they stood, foreheads resting on one another, breath coming in heavy gasps.

"I think I'd better go," Greg said. Yet he did not stir from his position, did not even shift a hand from Kim's waist. He was more confused than ever. Her reaction to his light kisses had moved so quickly from playful just-getting-to-know-you to sizzling emotional overload that he was unable to form any coherent thoughts. He needed a good night's sleep before he'd be able to do any thinking at all.

"I guess you'd better," Kim agreed. Reluctantly, she stepped back, releasing him and forcing him to do the same.

She stood at the door, watching as he climbed into the car and backed out of the driveway. The longing on her face almost made him slam on the gas and squeal down the street. But he managed to control himself, to not wake the entire neighborhood—and to leave himself more confused than ever.

Chapter Nine

Kim smiled across the bank counter at Emma. Holding Devin in her arms, Emma stood there grinning as she handed her deposit to Kim.

"So, how are you?" Emma's smile widened. "And how was the wedding in Hilo?"

Kim grimaced. She'd already been through some variation of this question a dozen times that morning. Even Greg's grandmother had been in, inquiring how the wedding had gone. She'd made a mysterious comment about Greg seeming troubled ever since he'd gotten back. It was a comment Kim wanted to spend time thinking over, but she'd been much too busy.

"I wish you'd come in an hour ago. I could have told you all about it over lunch."

Emma grimaced. "I know. I tried, but Devin really needed his nap and I didn't want to wake him."

Kim's hands stilled on the slips of paper in her hand. There was no one standing behind Emma, so it didn't matter if they took a moment to visit.

"It was a beautiful wedding. You should have seen the

gorgeous dress Crystal had. But the whole thing was still stressful, you know?"

"I'm sure."

"Crystal is the type who needs everything to be perfect," Kim continued, "so I wasn't surprised that everything was so nice. The gardens were beautiful. You'd think she'd ordered up all the blossoming flowers herself, because it made the air smell so good."

With a sigh, she checked the slips Emma had filled out and put the first one through the machine.

"Sounds pretty romantic."

"Oh, it was. But it wasn't *quite* perfect," she said. "It rained all day, just a quiet drizzle for the most part. But there was no sun, and the flowers, shrubs, and trees were all dripping." She frowned as she recalled the worry among the bridal party before they walked down the aisle.

"Did she have a tantrum?"

"No." Kim recalled Crystal's attitude about the rain, which had frustrated her deeply. But she'd acted surprisingly mature about it. "She pouted some, but for the most part she acted better than I expected. We'd all warned her about Hilo and its weather, so it's not like she didn't know. Heck, she's lived there for years."

Kim shrugged as she handed Emma her receipt. There was still no one else waiting for service, which was a good thing. Once again, she was the only teller working the window. But it also meant there was no one else waiting to pump her about attending her ex-boyfriend's wedding.

"Greg was wonderful," Kim went on, picking up the keys Emma had placed on the counter and shaking them in front of the baby. He reached for them with a big, happy smile. "I'm so glad we're friends again. It's a shame how many of our old friends we lose track of after graduation. Even my old roommates. I've been thinking that I really have to make more of an effort to keep in touch with Allison and Stacey."

Emma laughed even as she agreed. Forgetting the keys, her son looked up at her, then laughed too. "You're right. Of all the people in Malino, I'm certainly the one who should know about the importance of old friendships. Sometimes we *don't* lose touch with friends, and we *still* don't know what we have." She gave her friend a quizzical look. "Who knows, maybe you two were meant for each other. Look at me. I think everyone else in town knew before I did who my secret admirer was."

Kim tried to ignore Emma's hint as she dangled the keys in front of Devin once more. Emma and her husband, Matt, had been best friends throughout most of their lives, but had discovered their love only a few years ago. Kim did know that Emma was deliriously happy; but it was hard to see anything similar happening between herself and Greg. She'd noticed the distressed look in Greg's eyes whenever things seemed to get serious between them. And there was that disturbing comment his grandmother had made earlier that morning. Why would he be "troubled" unless he was having doubts about their relationship? If he'd been "troubled" since he got home, she had to conclude that their kisses had been more than he'd planned. Pushing their relationship to the next level was obviously more than he cared to handle.

Devin's hand closed over the keys, and Kim released them. He put them directly into his mouth. There was a boy who knew what he wanted. But Kim suspected Greg was not so decisive, at least where his personal life was concerned.

"He's a wonderful guy, Emma. We have fun together, and we found we actually have a lot in common. But I don't think he wants it to be anything more than that. He agreed to go to the wedding with me, because I was so desperate for a date, and we just kind of fell into doing other things together."

"Sure." Emma grinned. Pushing her receipt into her over-crowded bag, she shifted the baby in her arms. "That's why he arranged the birthday cake for you at the New Year's Eve celebration."

"Just friends," Kim reiterated. "Especially then. He's a really nice guy. But he gets kind of panicky whenever things get romantic."

"Aha! So things *do* get romantic when you're together," she said.

Kim frowned. "Just recently they have. But there's something bothering him, Emma, and I don't know what it is. Greg seems to be very nervous about us getting close. And since I don't know what the problem is, it's hard to address it. Did you ever hear anything about that girl who supposedly jilted him in Honolulu?"

Emma looked thoughtful. "From what I heard, he was pretty serious about someone he knew from the university. But when his mother got ill and he decided to come back to Malino, she dropped him. Apparently she didn't see herself married to a small-town vet."

"That's terrible." Kim felt her eyes tear up and blinked back the moisture. "No wonder he's scared."

Emma nodded just as Devin dropped the keys and began to squirm restlessly, peering down at the floor. Emma began to sway back and forth with him in the age-old dance of motherhood.

"I've got to get going. You'll figure it out," she said, stooping to retrieve the keys. "Just don't forget what I said about guys who are good friends. Things develop, you know? Nearness and all that. They get used to having you around, and don't like to do without."

While Kim still wasn't sure about this, she didn't contradict Emma. Things had certainly worked out well for her, and she'd insisted for years that she and Matt were nothing more than friends.

Kim was still thinking about this as she watched them walk out of the bank door. She was so deep in thought, she barely registered the entrance of Mr. Jardine until he stepped up to the counter and handed her a slip of paper.

Kim liked Mr. Jardine tremendously. He'd been a police officer for so many years that detecting still seemed an ingrained part of him, and she felt sure he had come in with the sole intention of learning more about her weekend.

"I need some new checks, young lady."

Kim took the form from him, quickly filling it out. She'd told him before that he could easily do it himself and mail it in, but she thought he enjoyed walking into town and visiting at the bank. Not to mention getting all the latest gossip while he was there. She hid a smile as she waited for him to ask about the wedding.

"And how are you doing, Mr. Jardine?" she asked.

"Just fine. Just fine," he said. "How is your fine mother?"

Kim talked about Paula for a few minutes, but she could see that Mr. Jardine was anxious to get on to other things.

"I'm glad to hear that she's doing so well," he said. "And how are *you* doing? How was that wedding on Saturday?"

Ah, the joys of small-town living, Kim thought. Everyone knew about Henry, of course, so everyone also knew about Crystal and Kim's presence in her wedding party. It was a good thing she'd gotten past the anger or she never would have made it through either the wedding or its aftermath.

"It was a lovely wedding, Mr. Jardine." Kim filed away his check order form and folded her hands on the counter in front of her. "They even had fireworks at the end of the evening, as the bride and groom were leaving."

"Fireworks. Now that's something we could have done for Ben and Mele," he said.

Kim could tell that he was sorry he hadn't thought of it in time. Then his eyes took on a speculative look, and he made the comment Kim had been expecting.

"I hear you took that nice young veterinarian."

"Greg Yamamoto," Kim said. "Yes, I did. I knew him in high school, you know."

"Did you?" Mr. Jardine gave her a searching look before he continued. "It's a real shame what that girl did to him, you know. Just told him all she wanted was a husband who could give her a nice life, but on Oahu, not the boonies of the Big Island."

Kim stared as she finally heard what she'd begun to suspect. Greg had been badly hurt, and now he shied away from all women.

Mr. Jardine was nodding sagely. "And just as he found out about his mother, too. Must have been real hard on him."

Kim wanted to hear more and had a million questions. But just then the bank door opened and another customer walked in. Mr. Jardine backed away from the window as Aunty Liliuokalani approached. Right behind her was Aunty Joy. Kim sighed quietly. All her regular customers were going to find some excuse to drop in today; they would all ask after herself and her mother, then go on to inquire about the wedding. And just when she was finally learning something that might help her sort out her relationship with Greg.

She smiled at Aunty Liliuokalani as she watched Mr. Jardine, with his intriguing knowledge of Greg, walk out the door. Sometimes she hated small-town life. She sneaked a peek at her watch. Just two and a half hours to go.

By the time she got home that evening, Kim's frustration was showing.

"Did you ever think of moving into Hilo?" she asked her mother, as they sat down to dinner together. "Or Kona?"

Her mother seemed surprised by the question. "Of course not. Why would I want to leave a nice place like Malino? I have my house here, and family and friends." She added a scoop of peas to her plate. "It's close to my job at the medical center, too."

"We have family in Hilo," Kim said. She took some peas too, even though she wasn't particularly hungry.

They had a lot of relatives in Hilo. There were numerous cousins there whom she'd visited during her years at the university. She wasn't especially close to any of them, but she'd never had a car while she was in Hilo and they would pick her up for trips to the beach or shopping. Luckily, the house she and her friends rented was close enough to the campus so she could walk or ride her bike to class.

But Paula was shaking her head. "It wouldn't be the same living in the big city."

Kim stifled her laughter. Hilo might be the only thing on their island—large though it was—that qualified as a city, but it was laughable when you compared it to Honolulu. Or to any of those cities she saw regularly on television and in movies—New York, Los Angeles, Las Vegas.

Kim pushed the food around her plate with her fork, lining up the peas in a row alongside the rice.

It would be nice to visit one of those mainland cities, she thought. Not to live there; she didn't want to leave Hawaii permanently. Never that. But she'd like to visit somewhere else sometime, just to see what it was like.

Maybe Las Vegas, with its glittering casinos and fabulous shows. Or San Francisco, where her friend Luana lived with her new husband.

Paula watched Kim play with her food, a worry line creasing her forehead. "What brought this on?"

Kim sighed. "Just everyone in town coming into the bank today to do some sort of business and ask how the wedding went."

"Well, it was the first day back after a three-day weekend," Paula said.

Kim just looked at her, one side of her mouth tipped downward.

Paula laughed. "So? What did you tell them?"

"I told them all that it was a lovely wedding."

"And?"

Kim sighed again. "And that Greg and I are just friends."

Paula's voice softened. "And you'd like to be more, wouldn't you?"

Kim was surprised but tried not to show it. Did mothers know everything?

"I would," she admitted. "But Greg doesn't."

Paula offered a sympathetic smile. "I heard you come in Friday night. Or Saturday morning, it really was. I heard some talking in the kitchen."

"Oh, dear, I'm so sorry we woke you."

"Don't worry about it." Paula let her fork rest lightly at the side of her plate. "I heard the car, and I thought it would be you. Mothers always sleep lightly when their children are out and about," she said with a wry smile. "And then I heard the kitchen door, so I knew you were safely home. But it took me a bit to get back to sleep, and so I heard your voices. Which were *not* loud enough to bother me," she added. "And then it was very quiet for a while."

Paula finished with a satisfied smile, filling her fork with rice and bringing it to her mouth.

Kim blushed, not sure what to say. She poked a piece of chicken with her fork and brought it to her mouth, chewing carefully so she didn't have to answer right away.

"I thought so." Her mother nodded. "You're a grown woman, Kim, and I don't like to interfere."

Still chewing, Kim groaned inwardly. Why did parents always say that when they planned to meddle?

"I just want you to know that I like Greg. He's a nice man. I would be very happy to have him for a son-in-law. I think Violet would like having you as a granddaughter, too."

Kim swallowed, then put her fork down at the side of her plate. She was no longer hungry, if she ever had been. Her stomach was fluttering in dismay at what she perceived as her mother's intrusion in her private life. And with the confusion she felt at the moment, she didn't want or need this.

"Mrs. Moniz was in the bank this morning."

Paula didn't seem surprised.

"She asked about the wedding and said something about Greg being troubled since he got back from it. I didn't know what to make of that."

Paula nodded wisely, but didn't comment.

"Well?" Kim asked. "What do you think it means?"

"It means," her mother told her, "that you have your work cut out for you. He's lost his girlfriend, his mother, had to readjust his career plans and move back to his hometown. He might not be ready to love again." Paula took a sip of her iced tea. "Yet."

Kim sighed. Just her luck. She finds a really nice guy, falls in love . . . and he's afraid to fall in love.

"He's never said anything about his girlfriend. I'm just

starting to hear about what she did to him." She poked at her fork, watching it push against the mound of rice she'd barely touched. "But what would his mother's death have to do with him being afraid to fall in love? It's not at all the same thing."

But Paula was already shaking her head in disagreement. "The pain of loss can be hard for people to cope with. Maybe even more so for a strong young man who thinks he should be able to make everything right. With Greg, his mother hid the truth from him, so he didn't have the time to come to grips with her illness beforehand. And then, just as he learned about her illness, the woman he loves tells him she doesn't love him after all. Violet said he was devastated."

Kim picked up her fork again, but put it back down almost immediately.

"He told me about how he'd researched grief, and found these stages that people go through. He said he thought I'd helped him reach the final one. Acceptance."

Paula saw a lot of grief working with the elderly patients at the health center. She knew all about the five stages.

"Yes, but those last two are tricky. Depression and acceptance can tangle, and he might have mistaken a stoic attitude for real acceptance. Being depressed—if he was—might play into that. And all that business with his ex-girlfriend and being in love. He's probably wondering if he ever was in love with her, maybe even what love is."

Kim pushed her plate away and stood. She was filled with a restless energy she didn't know how to expel. When she tried to help clear the table, she spilled half her uneaten food on the floor, where it was immediately pounced upon by the curious cats.

Paula took the dishes from her hands. "I'll clean up. Why don't you go for a walk? You could use some exercise after being cooped up inside the bank all day. And it's a nice night."

Kim quickly agreed. "That's a good idea, Ma." She gave her mother a quick hug. "Thanks. And leave the dishes in the rack. I'll dry them when I get back."

With a firm purpose in mind, Kim quickly changed into a warmup suit and tennis shoes. At the last minute, she grabbed her tennis bag too, which raised eyebrows when she passed through the kitchen on her way out. She forestalled questions by speaking first.

"I thought I'd use up some of this energy by hitting a ball against the backboard. Might even help my backhand," she finished with a grin.

Paula smiled. "Good idea. Have fun."

Kim set a fast pace on her way to the tennis courts at the high school. It was a clear night, chilly with lots of stars overhead, and perfect for a brisk walk.

She had the tennis courts to herself—no big surprise on a Tuesday evening in February. Slamming the ball against the wall felt good. She was filled with a restlessness she couldn't identify, but it seemed that some of it involved a vague anger that she could vent on a small yellow ball.

When she first heard Greg's voice, she thought she'd imagined it, conjured it up out of some deep-seated desire.

Until she heard it again, louder, calling her name.

Turning, she saw Greg standing in the shadows just beyond the court with the backboard.

"I thought it was you." He took a step forward.

He was dressed in gray sweats, and Kim suspected he'd been running on the high school track just beyond the tennis courts.

"Hi."

Kim suddenly found herself tongue-tied and shy. She, who never lacked for something to say.

"Nice night for some exercise," she finally said. A bit lame, she thought, bringing up the weather. But since at least half the anger she was trying to vent came from frustration over Greg's attitude, she thought it the safest avenue.

"Yeah. I was just over at the track, running."

Kim nodded. "I thought so."

"Practicing your volley?"

"I guess." She shrugged. "Mostly just expending some energy. I spent all day at work answering questions about Crystal's wedding."

Greg offered a sheepish grin. "Me too."

"Really?" Kim stepped closer, the tennis racquet hanging limp in her hand.

Greg nodded. "You're good for clinic business. Everyone in town must have brought in a pet for a checkup or some general disorder or other. And a chance to ask me about the weekend."

Kim sighed. "I'm sorry."

"No need. I enjoyed myself this weekend. And it wasn't that bad today either. Can't complain about all the new business."

His grin seemed infectious. Suddenly, the day's inquisition struck her as funny. She had just needed someone else to share it with.

"Want to go over to the Dairy Queen and have something to drink?" Greg asked. "Milkshakes?" he suggested.

Kim remembered the pleasant time they'd shared over milkshakes planning his grandmother's birthday party. She couldn't think of anything she'd like more, but she tried to be discreet in her answer. If he was wary of falling in love again because of a past bad experience, she didn't want to scare him off by appearing too eager.

"Why not?" she said. However, she did pack up her racquet and balls in record time.

They ordered chocolate milkshakes despite the cool evening air, then walked slowly back toward their neighborhood.

"Tell me about living in Honolulu," Kim asked.

To her surprise, Greg laughed. "Getting tired of the small-town atmosphere?"

Kim sighed. He was always good at reading her mind. He did it again this time, though imperfectly. She wanted to hear him say something about the woman who'd jilted him in his hour of need, not just hear how living in the city compared to living in a small town.

"Sometimes," she answered. "Like today. Everyone coming into the bank and pretending to do some type of business just so they could ask me about the wedding."

Greg worked to suck some of the thick shake through his straw before answering.

"I liked it in Honolulu while I was there. It's a big, exciting place for a young man on his own for the first time. I stayed at the dorm at first, then got a place with some other guys." He looked over at her and smiled. "Like you did."

Another thing they had in common, Kim thought. Though he'd heard all about her relationship troubles and she had yet to hear a word about his.

"I always thought I'd stay there after I graduated. I like working with the small animals—the cats and dogs and even birds. And I knew if I came back here there would be a lot of ranch and farm animals as well."

Kim let him talk, drinking her milkshake and walking quietly along beside him. He'd been gentlemanly enough to take her tennis bag, and it slapped along on his leg as they walked, making an even "thump, thump," like a cadence for a parade.

"Then when mom didn't come to my graduation, and I found out what was going on . . ."

Kim thought he might be biting his lip; he sounded faintly angry, yet making an effort to keep it under control.

"I couldn't believe she hadn't told me. I couldn't believe Dad and Vovo had kept her secret. I could have taken a year off. I could have come back and helped her."

"No." Kim's voice was firm, and it startled Greg into a stop. He stared down at her.

"What do you mean, 'no?' "

He sounded angry at her for disagreeing with him.

"Just what I said. No, you couldn't have helped her. Don't you see? That's why she didn't tell you. She knew you would postpone your education, and once you came back you might never go back. Didn't you have scholarships that helped with tuition? Would you have been able to count on keeping those if you quit?"

"It was a special case. I'm sure something could have been worked out."

"Get real, Greg. You know that kind of thing is wrapped in bureaucracy. You would never have gotten a sympathy vote from the red tape department. Your mother wanted what was best for you and she made her decisions accordingly."

They stood toe to toe on the side of the street, glaring at each other, mouths tight, until a car approached slowly. The headlights caught them in their bright light, embarrassing them enough to send them on their way again.

They walked in silence for half a block.

"You might be right," Greg finally said.

Kim didn't say anything, hoping that his statement would

help him settle things in his own mind. He'd stopped sipping his drink. Walking along and thinking things out apparently required his total concentration. She wondered if he would tell her now about that girlfriend. Or would she have to ask?

Kim could see the lights of her house up ahead. They could have been there ten minutes ago, but they'd walked around the long way instead of cutting through the backyards. It was better at night anyway, as long as you weren't trying to avoid letting everyone know where you were going and who you were seeing.

Kim knew they were well beyond sneaking around. She hoped this evening's walk wouldn't bring another onslaught of curious questioners to the bank. She was trying to decide just how to get him onto the subject she wanted to discuss when she heard him take a deep breath. Once again, it appeared he'd read her mind.

"There's something I want you to know."

Kim almost stopped, looking up at him. Without words, she urged him on by sending out good vibes and an understanding look.

"I had a girlfriend for my last year in school." He released a long breath, and avoided looking at Kim. "I thought I was in love. Now I'm not so sure."

Kim decided her best tactic was to remain silent and let him talk. She really needed this information, and she didn't want to say the wrong thing and have him close up on her.

Greg's steps slowed as he struggled with what he wanted to say. At this new pace, the tennis bag hung motionless at his side.

"Anyway, for a year I dated a woman I thought was the person I would spend the rest of my life with. She was beautiful and fun. She liked listening to my stories of the animals I treated. We had friends we socialized with. She was just as excited as I was when the clinic in Kailua offered me a position." He heaved a giant sigh. "Then, when I learned about my mother's cancer, and decided to come back here . . . then I suddenly realized I didn't know her at all. She screamed at me. Said I'd led her on and that she'd wasted a whole year with me."

Kim felt tears gathering in her eyes as she heard the hurt in his voice. She reached out and placed her hand on his arm, wanting to offer the comfort of her support. His voice droned on, emotionless. It broke Kim's heart.

"It turned out she never loved me after all. She wanted a husband who was a professional man, someone who would give her a good life, a nice house, and a way to get into the proper social circles."

Kim didn't know what to say. She was afraid any words of sympathy would be rejected as pity. And she could certainly understand that after her own experiences. So she said nothing.

As they walked up the gravel driveway at Kim's house, Greg slung the tennis bag from his shoulder, ready to pass it back into her possession. But he continued to hold on to it as they stopped at the kitchen door.

"I just wanted you to know where I'm coming from."

An infinite sadness clouded his eyes as he looked into her face. Was he searching for pity? Kim was determined that he wouldn't find any. Instead, she nodded.

"Thank you for sharing that." It seemed a lame thing to say after such an emotional exchange, but she didn't think he would want anything more, unfortunately. She'd love to comfort him, but he wasn't ready. Still, she felt impelled to offer.

"Do you want to come inside?" Kim asked.

"No thanks. I think I'll walk a little more. I have some thinking to do."

He finally passed the bag over to Kim. She hadn't even realized that they'd been holding it between them all that time.

"Thanks for listening."

"No," Kim protested. "That's what friends are for. And I should be thanking you," she added. "For carrying my bag. For buying the milkshakes."

But Greg shook his head. "No. That was nothing."

He leaned over and kissed her on the forehead. Like a sister, Kim thought in disgust.

"I'll see you later, Kim. Got a lot of thinking to do."

He walked off with his head low, sucking the last of the milkshake from the paper cup in his hand.

Chapter Ten

Greg must have had a whole lot of thinking to do. Kim didn't see him for the rest of the week. She didn't have time to pine, however. Malino was abuzz with news, and like everyone else, Kim was swept up into the excitement.

At the very moment that Kim had been lamenting to her mother that she was tired of small-town life, some of the local teens had been meeting with Reverend Charles. While she and Greg had walked home sipping their milkshakes, Reverend Charles had been conferring with the parish activities committee. The meetings had widespread repercussions throughout Malino. Happily for Kim, it knocked the subject of her relationship with Greg right off the Malino grapevine.

The teens at the local church had talked Reverend Charles into sponsoring a Mardi Gras party on the upcoming Shrove Tuesday. With just two weeks until the big day, everyone planned to pitch in. In the process, the party grew from a teen get-together to yet another town event. Since everyone was helping, they all planned to attend.

"Have you heard the latest?"

Kim was leaving the General Store when she almost ran into Emma and Devin coming in. The three of them stood bunched in the doorway until Mrs. Young hurried up to fuss over Devin and take him off for a cookie.

Kim and Emma moved into the store but remained near the door, talking.

"You mean the teens' Mardi Gras?" Kim's smile matched Emma's.

Emma nodded eagerly. Her eyes sparkled with merriment just thinking about it.

"Wouldn't it have been fun to have something like that when we were teens? Costumes and dancing—and all on a weekday night!"

Kim nodded. "Malino is definitely getting more exciting for young people. Now we have not only the Christmas party and the Kamehameha Day parade, there's the fireworks on New Year's Eve. But this Mardi Gras party! However did they get the old-timers to agree?"

Emma laughed. "My mother said it wasn't hard. They all like a good party as well as the next person. She said the only condition they had was that it should be for everyone in town, not just for the teens."

"From what I've been hearing, it's going to be crowded. Will the church's community room be big enough?"

"They have permission to use the high school gym if necessary," Emma said. "That's why they're asking people to pick up a ticket. There's no charge—though they will have a calabash at the door—but they need an idea of the numbers."

Kim nodded. It sounded like a good plan.

"I just got tickets for Mom and me from Mrs. Young," she said, shifting the plastic shopping bag from one arm to the other and patting it.

She glanced over at Mrs. Young, holding Devin on her

lap behind the counter. Feeling self-conscious, she looked back at Emma.

"So, what are you going to wear?" She shifted her weight from one foot to the other. "Do you think everyone will come in Hawaiian costumes, or will they go out and get neat-looking stuff?"

Emma had obviously already given this some thought. "I figure the little kids will use what they have from Halloween. The teens who wanted to have the dance are all involved in the high school drama club, so they might get more original. My cousin Sheila is one of them and she's not saying, so I have a feeling they're going all-out." Her gaze moved quickly over to her son then back to Kim. "It will be a lot of fun. I can't wait."

Kim gave her a wry look. "You still didn't say what you'll be wearing." A mischievous look sparkled in her eyes. "Come on, girl, spill. You're planning something."

They laughed together as Emma finally explained her costume idea and her reticence to mention it to anyone. She wanted to come as the main character from her husband's new video game. She was already working on the costume but trying to surprise Matt as well as everyone else; it was tough going.

"So you can't tell *anyone*, Kim. I mean it. Not even Greg. I'm working on it at Mom's house and hiding everything away every day, hoping that Matt won't walk in unexpectedly one morning or afternoon." She sighed. "It can be really hard to plan a surprise for your husband when he works at home."

Kim nodded absently. She was still thinking of Emma's warning not to tell anyone—"not even Greg." Why would she think it necessary to add that caveat? And so casually, as though they were an established couple. She'd admitted to Emma that she wished they were, but that was as far as it went. She'd had high hopes after he'd told her about his breakup with his last girlfriend. But then she hadn't seen him again.

Emma interrupted her disquieting thoughts.

"So now that you know, how about you? What will you wear?"

Kim frowned. "I've been thinking about it ever since I heard. Corinne talks about nothing else and even Nishiko mentioned the kimono she's going to wear. I have some old hula costumes I can dig out if that's what everyone is doing."

She looked uncertainly at Emma. "You're really going with an exotic video game costume, huh?"

Emma laughed. "Well, I don't know about exotic, but it is revealing. I'm a little worried about this stomach Devin left me with."

Kim looked down at her friend's flat stomach. "Oh, come on. You look great."

Emma glanced uncertainly at her midsection. "Well, it's not too bad in jeans, but a bodysuit is a whole 'nother thing."

She threw a look toward her son, happily munching another cookie in Mrs. Young's arms. Kim knew she didn't for a moment regret ruining her stomach muscles.

"So, come on. I told you my big secret, it's your turn. What will you wear? And forget the hula costume thing, all the old aunties will be wearing muumuus. You're too young for that."

Kim crinkled her nose at the thought of being lumped in with all the elderly matrons.

"Well, I couldn't come up with anything else, so I'm thinking of wearing the dress from Crystal's wedding. Greg made some comment about the lot of us looking like a bunch of wood nymphs or something. With the wedding in the gardens and all, you know? So that made me think of fairies, and I decided to make some wings." She held up the bag from the store. "I was just picking up some organza and wire to try and make some."

Emma's response was enthusiastic.

"That's a great idea. And don't forget to put glitter on them—that glitter glue will work. And make a floral wreath for your hair, one of those Renaissance Fair things with lots of trailing ribbons floating out in back."

Kim laughed at her friend's eagerness to help. "I haven't even decided if it will work."

"Of course it will." Emma dismissed her doubts with a careless flip of her hand.

"So Greg said you looked like a wood nymph, huh?"

Emma's eyes danced with merriment, but Kim could feel her cheeks flush with color. She'd had the same reaction when Greg had made the foolish remark. And it had been a lot more personal than she'd let on with her explanation to Emma.

"It was nothing. The dresses were very pretty, and the color, too, but it's so pale most of us looked very washed out. After everything I'd told him about Crystal, Greg decided she'd chosen the shade on purpose so that none of us would look better than she did."

Emma frowned. "You think?"

Kim shrugged. "Who knows? Crystal is certainly capable of doing that. The dresses were a pale apricot color, too much yellow in it to really look good on us Hawaiian and Asian girls. It looked best on Stacey, who's from the mainland. And I'm sure it would have been fabulous on Crystal. So she probably just chose it because she liked it and would have picked it for herself."

"So how'd he mention the wood nymph thing?"

Kim wasn't sure and said so. "Maybe he thought we looked like flowers hiding in the woods," she added.

"Or ripe fruits," Emma suggested, which sent them both off on fits of laughter.

On the other side of town, Greg was urging his father and grandmother to attend the Mardi Gras party.

"Sounds like a lot of foolishness," Frank said gruffly.

"Everyone is going. It will be fun," Greg insisted.

With no perceptible change in his father's attitude, Greg brought out the argument most likely to gain their acquiescence.

"Mom would have loved it," he said.

"You're right," Violet replied. "We should go, Frank. Remember, Reverend Charles did tell us to get involved with activities. He said that social and volunteer activities would be distracting. And that he was sure that was what Mary would have wanted. We should get involved with this."

Frank frowned. "But a costume party?"

Greg could hear the contempt in his voice. "Ah, come on, Dad, you know Mom would have loved it. I'll bet she'd have you all decked out like a cowboy or a pirate. And she would have made herself up like a saloon girl or a damsel in distress."

Frank continued to frown, but Greg could see that the edges of his mouth were working hard to retain that downward pull.

"You know he's right, Frank," Violet agreed. "Why, you can just wear some of your everyday work clothes, and put on a hat with a lei around the band, and you'll look like a *paniolo*." Frank wasn't really a cowboy, but his casual clothing could easily make him look the part.

"That's what I'm going to do," Greg said. "Want to take bets on how many of the men will turn up as *paniolos*?"

They all laughed. Neither of them would take him up on that losing proposition. Odds were ninety-nine to one that he was right.

"Will we be going with Paula and Kim?" Violet asked.

Greg tried to remain casual, but he had an idea his grandmother was on to him.

"I haven't asked her yet, but I was hoping to. You like going with Mrs. Ascension, don't you?"

"Yes. She's a lot younger than I am, of course, but she's a good woman. We both like to sew, too, and that gives us something to talk about."

"And you're both widows," he added.

"That too." Violet sighed. "The truth is, the older I get, the fewer of my friends are still around. I'll be going myself one of these days, so I try to enjoy what I have now."

"Vovo." Greg's voice came out stronger than he'd intended, and his grandmother startled. He gentled his voice and reached out to give her a hug. "I'm sorry, Vovo, I didn't mean to scare you. But I hate to hear you talk like that. You're going to be with us for a long time yet. You're only seventy-five. Aunty Liliuokalani is ninety and still going strong. And what about Mr. Jardine? Heaven knows how old he is—he looks about a hundred."

That made his grandmother laugh. "Oh, you," she chided him. But he could see the merriment in her eyes, and that was all he'd wanted.

"Come on. You help me get a box down from the hall closet. I have a real nice muumuu put away in there. I could wear it for the Mardi Gras."

Greg laughed. "Cowboys and hula girls, huh?"

"No, not a hula girl. Queen Kapiolani, maybe," she said with a regal shake of her head.

Greg obliged by laughing.

"I had a real nice black lace *holoku.* I don't even remember when I wore it last, for some function back when your grandfather was still alive."

She moved into the hall outside the bedrooms and opened the closet door.

"See, there it is," she said, pointing to a long box on the top shelf of the closet. "That's the box I want. I put some nice things away in there years ago."

Greg reached up, easily grasping the box and lifting it from the shelf. He carried it into the bedroom and placed it on her bed.

The strong smell of naphthalene flooded the room when she opened the box and peeled back the many sheets of tissue paper. Inside were the black *holoku* and what Greg realized must be his grandmother's wedding gown. He could see tears gather in her eyes as she parted the layers of tissue and looked at the white silk dress in the box.

Then she blinked hard, and quickly pulled out the black lace dress. Giving it a hard shake, she held it in front of her, turning toward the mirror over her dresser.

Greg stepped back, holding his nose in an exaggerated fashion that accomplished his purpose. It made her laugh.

"I think it will work. But you're right. It's going to need some heavy-duty airing."

She lay the black dress on the bed and took the white one from the box. Holding it up in front of her, she stood before the mirror once more. With a long sigh, she examined the yellowing silk.

"Can you believe I actually fit into this? Over fifty years ago . . ."

Greg watched his grandmother's eyes turn dreamy.

"It was right after the war and it was hard to get fabric. Especially white silk. But your grandfather knew a man who'd been a paratrooper and had a parachute. They made them out of silk back then, you know."

Greg didn't comment, but he knew it was a rhetorical question. She was back in her memories anyway, hardly aware of his presence.

"His friend had saved it for his own sweetheart's dress, of course. But then he came home and found she'd married someone else." She shook her head at the injustice of it. "So my Eddie offered him a horse for the parachute, and they made the trade."

Violet smiled, coming back into the present as she met her grandson's eyes in the mirror. "You're looking at a wedding dress that was made for the price of a horse."

"It's a beautiful dress, Vovo."

"Your mother wore it, too, you know."

That surprised Greg. How had he not known that?

"Really? I didn't know."

"Oh, yes. People weren't doing traditional weddings very much back in the seventies. If they even got married at all," she added with a disapproving sniff. "But my Mary liked tradition, and she wanted a church wedding and a proper wedding dress. She liked the idea of wearing my dress, and she and I were similar enough in build. I did make a few alterations, but not much."

"I wonder why I never knew about that." Greg said.

"Probably just because boys aren't as interested in those kinds of things. Maybe she never mentioned it; maybe you've just forgotten."

Greg nodded absently. He was watching his grandmother's face. She was still staring into the mirror, a rapt look of love in her eyes. What memories were stored in what amounted to a mere scrap of old and yellowing fabric? The dress was plain, too, nothing even remotely like the princess-in-the-fairytale dress Kim's friend Crystal had worn for her nuptials. He wondered if Crystal would look at her expensive confection of a dress this way, fifty-five years from now. Somehow he doubted it.

Seeing that Vovo was a million miles away, and happy there, Greg slipped silently from the room.

He'd been doing some profound thinking during recent days, and his grandmother had just helped him work out the last of his concerns.

With all that had happened to him in the past year, he'd become afraid. Afraid to get close to anyone other than his father and grandmother; it was already too late as far as they were concerned. But he didn't want to love anyone else. He didn't want to trust that he could determine who was worthy of his love. He didn't ever want to go through another episode like that final scene with Teri. The pain of ending a relationship was just more than he felt able to face again.

But then he'd found Kim. Or, more properly, she'd found him at the Malino Christmas party. And in spending time with her—casual time, doing everyday activities—he'd come to be very fond of her. So fond that he began to fear he was falling in love. Something he'd sworn he'd never do again. He spent sleepless nights thinking about her, about the person she seemed to be. And he debated whether she was truly the person he saw. And whether he could trust his judgment after his disaster with Teri.

In the past week, he'd been reconsidering. Romantic love was supposed to be the biggest thing anyone could ever find. He'd certainly been happy for most of his time with Teri. He thought she had been as well. Should he decide that he would never experience love just because the pain of losing Teri and his mother had been so devastating? That particular set of circumstances would never occur again, of course, but his self-confidence was so shaken that he found himself unable to come to a decision.

Tonight's sight of his grandmother looking into the mirror at her wedding gown had been the clincher. Her eyes had filled with tears looking at the yellowing dress, yet he could see the joy that came with those tears. She'd lost her husband many years ago, she'd lost her only daughter. But she wasn't remembering the pain of loss, or even the daughter who'd shared the dress. She was recalling the love they'd shared, the beautiful family they'd been, and the good years they'd all had together. If he'd wondered if love was worth it, he could now say for sure that it was.

Greg barely registered the basketball game that was on as he joined his father in front of the television.

"Vovo okay?" Frank asked. He was watching the basketball game and reading the newspaper.

"She's good. She's going to air out the *holoku*."

His father grimaced. "Good. I could smell it in here. I hope the place airs out before bedtime."

"Maybe I should get the fan," Greg suggested, but his father waved him back into his seat.

"Leave it. It'll be fine." He returned his attention to the newspaper.

"Her wedding dress was in the box with the *holoku*," Greg said. He was interested to see what his father's reaction would be.

He didn't have to wait long. The newspaper sagged in Frank's hands, whatever he'd been reading forgotten. The television could have been turned off. His eyes seemed focused on the screen, but it was obvious to Greg that he was looking inward.

"Did you know Mom wore Vovo's wedding dress?"

"Oh, yes. Your mother was very proud of that." A smile

transformed his father's face. He folded the paper onto his lap, the day's news forgotten. "I haven't thought about that for years. It was white silk, made from a World War II parachute."

Greg had to smile at the happy look in his father's eyes. "Obtained in barter for a horse," he added, a mischievous smile on his lips.

Frank laughed. "Oh, yes, that was a story your grandfather loved to tell. I heard it many times. The silk fabric was starting to yellow, and your mother and grandmother washed it by hand and then laid it on the grass in the sun to bleach it out." He shook his head, lost in his memories. A faint smile touched his lips. "It worked too. She looked so beautiful, coming down that aisle . . ."

As Greg had seen his grandmother's do in the bedroom a few minutes earlier, his father's eyes clouded, turning dreamy. But, like his grandmother, his father's face showed no grief, just the happiness of love and beautiful memories. It brought to mind the discussion he'd had with Kim on the drive home from Hilo. These stories they were sharing about his mother; they weren't making anyone cry. On the contrary, these were happy memories, bringing only smiles and joy.

And now Greg knew. He'd been wrong these past months. He'd been trying to keep himself aloof, trying hard not to let anyone penetrate his new protective shell. He'd thought that by remaining detached he could isolate himself from facing more pain.

But a certain young woman had managed to get close anyway, making him forget his pain, making him laugh without guilt, making him look forward to life again. He wondered how he could ever have thought that she wasn't the genuinely caring person she seemed to be.

A vague plan that had taken root in his mind suddenly

demanded attention. It was a romantic thought, one he'd refused to acknowledge until now. At the Christmas party, a lot had been said about the romanticism of Ben's actions. Kim and all the women had been touched by this. It was the factor that was most often mentioned as they wiped the tears from their eyes. It was so romantic.

While his father continued looking back on his years of marital happiness, Greg looked forward. Perhaps he could create something romantic for Kim. Not in front of the whole town; he didn't think he could manage that. But something special she could remember when she was Vovo's age.

The basketball game played on, but neither of the men sitting in front of the television noticed.

The "Malino Mardi Gras" was held at the high school gym. The local teens decorated with miles of crepe paper streamers in purple, gold, and green; they even managed to acquire several boxes of tawdry beads in the same colors to pass out at the door. The school's drama club, the same group who'd lobbied for the party, greeted arrivals in the gym's narrow lobby, charming everyone with their elaborate medieval costumes. The Mardi Gras idea was apparently an elaborate advertisement for their upcoming production of "Romeo and Juliet." Greg had to shake his head at the advertising acumen of today's teenagers.

By the time he and his family entered the main area of the gymnasium, the room was filled with milling, costumed people. *Paniolos*, too numerous to count, mixed with hula girls and belly dancers, vampires and brides. Music blared from the school's sound system. One area had been designated for dancing, but so far no one had ventured onto the floor.

As Greg had begun to plan his actions for the evening,

he'd decided against inviting Kim and Paula to join them. So his eyes scanned the room eagerly now, hoping to see Kim. When he did not, he played the gallant and escorted Vovo over to join her friends.

Leaving her blushing over the many compliments coming her way, he then took the basket she held from her hands and started over to the refreshment table. The Mardi Gras party was not supposed to include a meal, but food of some kind was deemed a necessity, and the attendees all arrived laden with contributions.

A typical Hawaiian party, Greg thought with a smile as he approached the table, his stomach already rumbling in anticipation of some of the delectable-looking choices. Not unexpectedly, there was a preponderance of *malasadas*, because Shrove Tuesday was known as Malasadas Day among the island Portuguese. The holeless donuts overflowed from plates and baskets, but there were also plates filled with cookies and slices of quick breads, bowls of *poke* and potato chips, even a platter of *lumpia*. No one would ever starve at a Malino party.

Greg had just deposited his grandmother's basket of *malasadas* on a table when he turned and saw her. She was like a woodland vision, stepping out of a crowd of people rather than shrubs and tree trunks. He smiled when he recognized the apricot dress. But what a difference! She'd done something to the color of it; it was now a rosy pink at the neckline that faded out to the familiar golden apricot at the hem. It held all the colors of a ripe peach, and no longer leached the color from her face, instead making her cheeks glow. A wreath of pink and yellow orchids sat in her hair, with long narrow ribbons in pink, peach, apricot and gold trailing out behind her—over small translucent fairy wings!

The sight of Kim as a woodland fairy hit Greg square in

the chest. His heart clenched so tightly that he wondered if he might be having a heart attack, until he recognized it for what it was—the fact that a beautiful woman had captured his heart. And he hoped she continued to do so.

He smiled in anticipation. This was going to be an evening to remember.

Kim stepped into the gym, filled with apprehension. Disappointed that Greg had not called and issued an invitation for her to join his family, she had come with Emma, Matt, and Sonia. And Devin, of course. The baby looked very sweet in a tiny aloha shirt that matched his dad's. Emma, however, was turning heads with her outfit. And poor Matt could barely stand to tear his eyes from her. To say he'd been thrilled to see his creation come to life was to understate the matter enormously.

Kim was glad they'd all come together. With the attention Emma was drawing, she felt no one would notice her outfit. Paula and Emma both thought her costume inspired, and Sonia had raved over it. But she remained filled with doubt. Emma was her best friend and Sonia was an artist. The outfit was too sophisticated for Malino—she almost giggled at the thought of herself as sophisticated—but the elegant Crystal had chosen the dress, hadn't she? Perhaps she herself had become sophisticated by association.

Kim clung to the plate of brownies she'd brought to the party. Having foreseen the avalanche of *malasadas*, she'd gone for chocolate, making a large double batch. She'd filled her largest platter with them, so that she would have a big object to cling to—or hide behind—in case her costume provoked giggles.

As she approached the food table, she felt a strange prickling at the back of her neck. Someone was watching her. Kim wasn't sure she'd ever had such a presentiment before, but she was sure of it at that moment. Someone was not only watching, but staring at her.

She turned slowly, almost afraid that she would see someone pointing, a smirk on his or her face. But instead, her eyes locked on Greg's. He stood a mere ten feet away, his eyes drinking her in. And he wasn't smirking, wasn't laughing. In fact, his expression was almost stunned.

Taking a deep breath, Kim stepped forward. She had to leave her platter on the table, and Greg was standing right beside it.

"Hello," she said, and immediately grimaced. *Of all the awkward, insipid openings . . .*

"Hello yourself."

It seemed like forever since she'd seen him, and Kim could hardly control her reaction. Her heart was pounding, her blood running rapidly through her veins. She was sure her cheeks wore bright circles of color.

"You did something to the dress."

Still clutching the heavy platter, Kim nodded. If possible, her heart rate increased even more at this indication of his awareness of her. "Mrs. Young suggested it. I used fabric paint, and touched it up a little."

Greg nodded, but she noticed that, after his initial perusal, his gaze remained locked on her face, examining her, as though trying to pull the very thoughts from inside her head.

"So . . ."

After what seemed like minutes but was surely just seconds, he nodded toward her hands. "I see you brought chocolate."

Startled into action, Kim scolded herself for mooning, and placed the large dish on the table.

"Chocolate is always good," she said, busying herself with removing the plastic wrap and folding it into a small square, which she finally pushed under the table. The hanging plastic tablecloth would hide it from view, and someone might need it afterward, when they were gathering up leftovers to take home.

As Kim stood, deliberately facing the table, hoping to regain her composure, she felt Greg's arm brush against hers as he reached for a brownie. She knew it was his arm, even without seeing anything more than half a sleeve and a large hand. No one else's brief touch could make her whole body hum with awareness. Closeness to another man had never brought this flooding warmth that flowed through her body from the point of impact.

When she finally turned around, Greg remained right beside her. He was calmly chewing the last of his brownie, licking the last bit of chocolate from his fingers with evident enjoyment.

Kim bit her lip, swallowing hard, as she watched his mouth move.

It took her a moment to realize that he was speaking to her.

"Want to dance?"

Kim looked quickly around the room. There were a few people on the dance floor. Many more were standing around the edges of the room, eating and visiting and admiring the parade of costumes.

It was a rock song, and the dancers were mostly teens, including a couple in beautiful velvet medieval garb. But she decided she didn't care if she looked like an old lady out there, she wanted to remain with Greg. And perhaps the next song would be a slow one, and she would have a legitimate reason to be in Greg's arms.

As they walked the short distance to the dance floor, Kim was amazed that Greg was asking her to dance. She knew from the wedding reception that he wasn't fond of dancing.

The tune ended just as they stepped onto the dance floor, and they faced each other awkwardly, Kim wondering if she should turn and leave the dance area. But Greg asked her to wait, and—joy of joys—the next number was an old one, slow enough for close dancing.

Walking into Greg's arms, Kim shut her eyes and relaxed into the moment. What a delight to be there, right where she wanted to be. His arms were strong and supporting. Yet they held her gently, making her feel like a precious object held under his protection.

Greg moved into the rhythm of the music with more confidence than he'd ever felt. It was as though he'd come home. This was what he wanted. This was what he needed. Kim in his arms, Kim in his life.

With a new assurance in his ability, he moved boldly with the music, feeling Kim respond to his lead. After a minute he felt her head come up off his chest, and looked down to see her peering up at him, a smile on her face, happiness in her eyes.

"Have you been taking dancing lessons?"

"No. I've just been inspired tonight by a certain woodland fairy."

Greg knew his words, fanciful as they seemed, were true. He'd had a difficult week. He'd made the decision to stay away from Kim while he worked things out, because he knew he had to do it himself. Being around her would influence him in ways he couldn't allow while he made life-altering decisions.

When he'd seen her tonight, he knew he'd made the proper decision. The instant physical reaction he'd had; it was that kind of response to her that had worried him, made him afraid he would not be able to think rationally if she was near.

Not only that, the impact of seeing her in her costume for the first time, as she stepped from the crowd, was worth the agony of not being with her for so long.

His week of heavy thinking had not been easy. He'd spent hours each night working out, letting the physical activity tire him while his mind grappled with his reaction to Kim and what he wanted to do about it. He'd had to face up to his insecurities, issues that ran back to his teen years. It hadn't been easy.

In the end, he'd decided to go for it. He'd even driven out to Ben Mendoza's ranch to confer with him about love and marriage. And courage, and romantic proposals.

So he'd arrived at this moment—ready to risk everything for a chance at the kind of love his parents and grandparents had experienced. He was trusting himself, trusting in Kim.

Greg took a deep breath. Here he was, at the Mardi Gras dance, a beautiful Kim in his arms. An expensive ring in his pocket.

Chapter Eleven

Kim raised her head and smiled up at Greg. She'd been dancing with her eyes closed, her cheek resting lightly against his chest. It was pure bliss.

"What are you thinking?"

Greg smiled. He wanted to tell her, but he'd made plans. Romantic plans.

"Did you know they're planning prizes for some of the more special costumes?"

Kim nodded.

"I think you'll take a prize without any trouble."

She smiled up at him. "Oh, Greg."

There was definitely something there in her eyes. Love, he thought. He hoped.

They danced one song after another, enjoying the pleasure of being together during the slower ones. Unfortunately, there weren't nearly enough of those.

At eight-thirty, the families with young children began to leave. At nine, the drama club teens took over the microphone to announce the presentation of leis for the most unusual or most impressive costumes. They had waited until the children left so as not to make it too much like Halloween and confuse the little ones.

"Can you believe there's a panel of judges?" Kim asked. She was having trouble not laughing over the pretension of it all. The teens who had instigated the dance were the judges, of course. And going up on stage to make the announcements gave them more of a chance to show off their own beautiful outfits—and another opportunity to advertise their play.

"I think it was a good idea," Greg said. "Just think of the problems if they tried to have a popular vote."

Kim shuddered just thinking about it. Everyone would vote for their relatives or themselves. No one would get overwhelming support, and there would be lots of hard feelings. It was the kind of thing that would cause sisters not to speak to each other for years.

"You're right. What was I thinking?"

They laughed as someone put on "When the Saints Go Marching In."

"The kids really did their research," Kim said. "They seem to have all the right touches for the Mardi Gras and New Orleans."

"With island touches," Greg said, thinking of all the *malasadas* on the snack table, and the ti-leaf leis on the arms of the presenters. "No beignets or pralines."

To Greg's regret, Kim was not one of those presented with a lei. But her friend Emma was, blushing prettily in her red body stocking with a little pleated skirt and white boots that represented the star of Matt's latest computer game.

"Another advertisement," Greg whispered to Kim, and they both laughed.

"Everything is so commercial nowadays," Kim agreed, but she cheered heartily for her friend anyway.

When Violet was called up, "in her beautiful Queen Emma gown," Greg felt his throat tighten so much that he was barely able to speak. But he managed to tell Kim that she'd be irritated about that later, as she was supposed to represent Queen Kapiolani. Still, she accepted her lei with dignity, and smiled benevolently at everyone as she left the stage.

Several others were called up for special costumes, many of the older men and women wearing beautiful ethnic costumes—kimonos, Filipina dresses with stiff ironed sleeves, and even one man in a samurai warrior's costume.

Once the presentations were over, the lights were dimmed, and more couples headed to the dance floor. Greg offered his hand to Kim once again. Any awkwardness he'd felt about his abilities as little as two weeks ago was past; perhaps he'd just needed the proper partner all along.

As they moved into place, Greg looked over to the young man at the CD player and nodded. Then he took Kim into his arms and began to move.

"Remember when we first met . . . at the Christmas party? After Ben proposed?"

Kim smiled, her face radiant with the memory. "Who could forget?"

"Everyone that night kept talking about how romantic it all was."

Kim laughed softly. "Except you. You just couldn't believe he had enough courage to propose in front of the whole town."

"Everyone kept talking about romance, and I was running scared."

Kim opened up the space between them so that she could look up into his face. "Were you?"

"Oh, yes." He swallowed. Just because he'd made his decision didn't make acting on it any easier.

"I have a lot of insecurities left over from my teenage years, when I was the clumsy nerd with little athletic talent. And then there was the number Teri did on me. I lost most of my self-confidence along with her," he admitted.

Kim continued to look up at him, her heart in her eyes. At least, that's what he thought. That's what he hoped.

"I can't believe how lucky I was to run into you that night, Kim. Doubly lucky that you needed a date for a wedding and chose to ask me."

Her lips were moving into a smile, but he had to pull himself away from thoughts of that. Looking at her lips just led him to want to kiss her, and that would have to wait. He needed to say all he had to say. He had plans for the next song, and it would be coming up soon enough.

"You've saved me from becoming a bitter and lonely old man, Kim."

Although his words were serious, he realized how silly they sounded when Kim laughed.

"Yeah, I can see how old you are," she said.

Greg's grin was rueful. "I guess that wasn't quite what I wanted to say. What I meant was that I would have ended up that way—all alone because I was too afraid to love again. Maybe too insecure to think that someone would love me. I was heading toward being an eccentric old man with a house full of dogs and cats and no family of his own."

Kim was still smiling. "Okay. I can see you like that. The crazy old coot down the street."

He had to laugh with her. "But I'm not going to be that crazy old coot," he declared.

As one song ended and another began, Greg stepped away from her, still holding her hand. He'd thought of going down on one knee, the way Ben had, but he couldn't quite do it. He wanted a romantic episode for Kim, but some things were just too much.

The voice of Frank Sinatra poured out of the sound system, singing "Our Love is Here to Stay," the song he'd requested the deejay segue into after his signal.

He held Kim's hand, gazing deeply into her eyes.

"I asked for this song, Kim. It was a difficult choice, between this and 'Unforgettable.' You see, no matter what you say here tonight, I'll never forget you. And, as the song is saying, I'll always love you."

He brought her hand up to his mouth, placing a soft, light kiss on the back of it. Even as he looked deep into her eyes, his left hand fumbled in his pocket for the jeweler's box.

"Kim, will you make me the happiest man in the world and be my bride?"

Kim stared at him, speechless. His hand holding the small velvet box, remained at his waist. His heart had stopped beating. His throat constricted; soon he wouldn't be able to breathe at all. He was sure she meant to turn him down.

Then he saw her blink. And blink again. Something sparkled on her eyelashes. Did she have glitter in her mascara?

Then Greg realized what he was seeing, and his hopes soared. She was crying. Or fighting tears. Did she mean to accept?

His hand tightened on hers, pulling her closer. He raised the jeweler's box up so that she could see it.

She didn't. They were both so wrapped up in looking into each other's eyes that Greg would have missed her words if not for seeing her lips move.

"Yes. Oh, yes."

Then she flung herself at him, throwing her arms around

his neck. He caught her close and spun her around the floor, too happy to even notice the strange looks coming from the other couples on the dance floor.

Finally, he stopped spinning, put Kim down, then kissed her soundly. By now, no one was dancing. Everyone stood, many still arm in arm, watching the couple "going a little nuts," as Mr. Jardine was heard to say.

Greg proffered the velvet box.

"I got this for you, but you can exchange it if you don't like it."

Slowly, Kim took the box, and gingerly opened the lid. Everyone knew what was happening now, so the crowd closed in. All the women were especially interested in seeing what was inside the small velvet box.

"Oh!"

Kim's gasp was completely swallowed by the larger one from the women around her. Those who couldn't see tried to push forward.

Nestled in the blue velvet box was a diamond solitaire ring. But it wasn't a plain ring with a boring gold band. In the tradition of Hawaiian heirloom jewelry, this ring's band displayed the swirls and twists of petals and leaves that were island flowers.

As she threw her arms around Greg once more, Kim could no longer stop the tears. As Greg took the ring from the box and put it on her finger, her other hand swiped at her cheeks.

"It's perfect, Greg. I love it."

She peered at the ring on her finger, a blissful smile on her face, happy tears still streaming down her cheeks.

After another soul-searing kiss, they became aware of the crowd around them. The whisperings were getting louder, the smiles and winks broader. Greg and Kim looked around at the press of people, then quickly back at each other. She blushed prettily, but Greg found he was not the least embarrassed.

"She said yes," he shouted. "We're getting married!"

The young man acting as deejay turned on his microphone. The song had been over for at least a minute, not that anyone had noticed.

"That last song was Frank Sinatra singing 'Our Love is Here to Stay,' played at the special request of Dr. Greg Yamamoto, and dedicated to his future bride, Miss Kim Ascension."

Applause rocked the gym, and Kim and Greg were swamped by well-wishers. Among the first were Ben and Mele Mendoza.

Ben slapped Greg on the back while Mele hugged Kim.

"Pretty romantic, I'd say," Ben told him. "Brave even." They shared a grin.

Kim heard the last, and smiled at her new fiancé. "We women here in Malino are really lucky. No one can top our local guys for romance."

"Hear, hear," shouted several of the women. Loudest of all were Mele and Emma.